BOOK 1

'YOU'RE SUCH A LITTLE FOOL YOU DON'T REALIZE THAT IF YOU STAY HERE YOU'RE GOING TO DIE!"

At first Lara doesn't believe the warning. Having come to Collinwood as Quentin Collins' guest, she falls in love with his cousin Barnabas, despite rumors that Barnabas is a vampire.

Wanting to be near Barnabas, she trusts him to keep her safe. But then a girl a killed, her throat torn out by a savage beast – possibly a werewolf. And Lara finds a death charm placed on her bed – a dead bat in a circle of blood.

Lara has been marked for death . . . by a killer whose supernatural powers may prove greater than Barnabas' own!

Hermes Press

Published by Hermes Press, an imprint of
Herman and Geer Communications, Inc.

Daniel Herman, Publisher
Troy Musguire, Production Manager
Eileen Sabrina Herman, Managing Editor
Alissa Fisher, Graphic Design
Kandice Hartner, Senior Editor

2100 Wilmington Road
Neshannock, Pennsylvania 16105
(724) 652-0511
www.HermesPress.com; info@hermespress.com

Book design by Eileen Sabrina Herman
First printing, 2020

LCCN applied for: 10 9 8 7 6 5 4 3 2 1 0
ISBN 978-1-61345-227-1
OCR and text editing by H + G Media and Eileen Sabrina Herman
Proof reading by Eileen Sabrina Herman and Feytaline McKinley

From Dan, Louise, Sabrina, and Jacob for D'zur and Mellow

Acknowledgments: This book would not be possible without the help and encouragement of Jim Pierson and Curtis Holdings

Printed in Canada

BARNABAS COLLINS AND QUENTIN'S DEMON
by Marilyn Ross

CONTENTS

CHAPTER 1

The haunting waltz seemed to follow her wherever she went. Lara Balfour stood alone in a shadowed corner of the big main salon of the coastal steamer, Governor Dare, and listened to the plaintive strings of the violin played by the small Italian lad who was one of the passengers. The youngest son of a family bound for Bangor to begin life in the New World, he had caught the attention of those on the side-wheeler almost as soon as the great white ship had left Boston Harbor.

The soulful eyes in the dark-skinned young face and the even teeth revealed by his quick smile, and his musical ability, made him a favorite with the passengers. In the early part of the day he had played lively airs on deck and passed his cap for tips. Now that it was long after midnight he still played but in a different mood. He caressed the strings of his violin to bring forth soft, relaxing music for the weary people on board.

And as he stood in the center of the salon a good portion of the passengers remaining on the ship gathered to listen to him. Lara was among this group. The ship would stop next at the village of Collinsport and she would get off, not sorry to end the long journey. The rhythmic threshing of the giant side-wheels pounded in her brain. And there had been a thunderstorm which had now turned to a drizzle of rain. Not a pleasant welcome for her arrival at the small

Maine seaport.

As she had stood with the others listening to the lad play he had all at once embarked on this waltz which her father had written. It had caught the popular fancy among all his other melodies and even this youth from a foreign land had somehow heard it and was playing it to amuse the passengers.

She wore a wistful smile on her piquant oval face, thinking what a stir there would be among those gathered around the violinist if they knew she was the daughter of the man who had composed it.

And it was this musical composition of her father's which had brought her on this journey to Collinsport to spend the summer at the home of Quentin Collins, who had been among the first to write her father and congratulate him on the waltz. He spoke of having purchased one of the first roll records of the piece and endlessly playing it on his gramophone. This had amused Lara at the time, for her father would not have one of the new mechanical music reproducers in his home. The fact that his music had been among the early numbers recorded had done nothing to change his mind.

"I detest those tiny monsters with their great horns," he had informed her. "It is a variety of bug I want no part of!"

Lara was used to her father's moods but she had encouraged him to continue a correspondence with Quentin Collins, who wrote him a series of eager letters concerning his many musical compositions. Illness had confined her father to their home in Philadelphia and he needed something to take up his time and interest. Her father grudgingly agreed and wrote Quentin Collins regularly.

When the letters from Quentin arrived, her father always summoned her to sit by him in the comfortable living room of the big brick house on Walnut Street while he read the letters aloud. Occasionally he would pause to comment on them.

"A remarkably sensitive young fellow," he said on one of these occasions. "He understands my music as well as any of the critics. And he is especially fond of my new waltz." Her father, a thin, austere man, paused for a bleak smile. "And now he has begun asking about you."

Lara blushed. "Why should he be interested in me?"

"I think the way he phrased it was, to inquire if you were as lovely as my music." He chuckled. "I told him you had inherited your late mother's fragile beauty. That you were as blond as I am now gray, medium of stature with a fine figure, and possessed earnest gray eyes set in a face of even beauty and of demure expression."

It was her turn to laugh. "I'm sure he thought you were indulging in a song lyric rather than a description of me."

Her father had regarded her fondly. "On the contrary, I would say I gave him only a true picture of you. It worries me that you are confined here taking care of me rather than mixing with people your own age and enjoying the male admiration you so richly deserve."

"Nonsense," she'd protested. "Being able to nurse you makes me happy."

Her father's thin face had shadowed. "But when I am gone you will be so alone. I worry about you a great deal. You will find it difficult to build yourself a new life."

She had refused to listen to him, as she always did when he began to talk in that fashion. The thought of her father's impending death was too frightening to contemplate. And when the end came a few months later she was shattered by her loss. It was then that young Quentin Collins had begun writing directly to her.

She had first written him of her father's passing as soon as she was well. Several letters addressed to her parent had meanwhile piled up. In her sorrow she'd written, "I will always appreciate your deep interest in my father's music and your kindness in writing to him. And I shall always think of the waltz you enjoyed so much as the waltz of Quentin Collins."

Her letter brought a prompt reply from the young man. "I only regret that problems here at Collinwood keep me from making a journey to Philadelphia," he wrote. "I would so much like to meet you in person and talk to you of your father's work."

She'd replied by thanking him and explaining that she had been ill. Because of that she went on to say, "I am not looking forward to the humidity and wicked heat of this city in the months ahead."

Quentin Collins had then sent her the first of his several invitations. "You would be a most welcome guest at Collinwood. My brother and I would try to make your stay here pleasant. And my Great-aunt Erica and her youthful companion, Catherine Edmonds, would offer interesting feminine company. Please give this invitation serious thought."

Lara had. It was 1895 and social conventions were not nearly as stuffy as they once had been. People would not think it strange of her to visit this fine young man, since he had been a long-time correspondent of her late father, and especially since he had suitable chaperones in his home. The invitation was tempting and yet she put it off.

The letter that came in mid-May had a tone of urgency different from the others. In it Quentin wrote, "I have been rather unwell lately myself, so it would be a great kindness to me if you would come and visit Collinwood. I know having you here would do wonders in restoring my health. And I think our Maine salt breezes and pleasant sunshine would be beneficial to you. We have a fine coastal boat service linking us directly with Boston. Its one disadvantage is that it arrives here late at night, but that is no real problem. I can meet you at the wharf and have you back to Collinwood in a carriage in no time."

The mention of his own poor health had touched her. It seemed so generous of him to concern himself about her when he was unwell. He had not mentioned the type of illness bothering him and though she searched in all his other letters she found no hint of the malady in them either. But the last letter did decide her to take advantage of his generous offer.

As she sat down to write him of her decision a gentle smile crossed her lovely face. For she realized that she had formed an interest for this man she'd never met as strong as that she felt for any of her friends in Philadelphia. It would be absurd to label her feelings as romantic, yet they must surely fringe on that. She was so lonely, as her father had warned she would be, that this link with her dead parent seemed a natural one. All at once she knew how badly she wanted to meet and know Quentin Collins.

All these thoughts passed through her mind as she stood in the soft lamplight of the red-carpeted salon and heard the Italian boy finish her father's waltz. There was a ripple of applause from the group in the salon and the dark lad shyly moved among them with his cap held out for coins. Lara fumbled in her purse and had some silver ready when he came up to her. She offered him a smile of encouragement and told him, "You play beautifully," as she placed the coins in his cap.

He smiled at her in return and quickly moved on to a bearded man on her right. Lara's attention was taken by the ship's horn blowing mournfully. The long journey had taught her this was a signal they were nearing one of the many stops. And this time the seaport would be her destination.

Braving the drizzle of rain, she left the warmth of the salon to go out on deck, surprised to discover that the big side-wheeler was very close to the Collinsport wharf. She could plainly see the blazing torches set out to light the operation of docking. And in spite of the darkness and wet mist she was certain she could pick out the figures of men standing on the wooden pier as they waited for the vessel to come close.

There were loud shouts from the deckhands as they made preparations for bringing the Governor Dare up to the wharf. The giant side-wheels made less noise and caused less vibration as they slowed. Lara leaned against the rail and peered into the night, wondering where Quentin Collins might be and what their first moment of meeting would be like.

Confusion was growing on the deck as many prepared to

land. She had already tipped the purser and arranged with him to see her luggage was safely put ashore. So now she waited only for the vessel to be tied to the wharf and the gangplanks set out before she went down to below decks and walked onto land again.

She clutched her purse to her and made her way down to the crowded area near the gangplanks. Everyone seemed eager to get off the vessel at once. The murky storage area of the side-wheeler was rich in a mixed smell of engine oil, molasses, tobacco smoke and the perspiration of the hard-working deckhands. Lara hoped that she soon might be freed from the pushing group which surrounded her. There was laughter and impatient comments from those waiting with her.

Then all at once everyone moved forward and she nearly stumbled as she stepped up on the wide planks leading steeply to the wharf itself. In a moment she was standing in the drizzle, breathing the fresh air and grateful for her escape from the crowd. Now she was faced with a new problem, that of finding Quentin Collins.

She stood rather anxiously, hoping that every person coming up by her might be her host. One rather elderly man came forward with a smoking lantern held in his hand. He gave her a searching glance.

"You be the parson's sister?"

She shook her head. "No."

The old man scowled and moved on without another word. Maine folk were not given to being talkative, someone had warned her. Gazing around her, she saw that most of the people on the wharf were already dispersing. They had been greeted by waiting friends or relatives and were going off to the carriages lined up on the hilly street above the wharf. But there still had been no sign of Quentin Collins!

She began to experience an odd fear. She recalled his mention of being ill and a tiny panic rose in her at the thought he might have taken a turn for the worse or even have died. It was a dreadful possibility; she didn't dare think what would happen if this were the case. She was sure from the tone of his letters that Quentin would never deliberately allow her to arrive without being properly greeted.

The Governor Dare let off a blast of her horn that made her start with shock. Her nerves were jumpy. The great side-wheeler would be away from the wharf in a few minutes and she would be left stranded in this strange place alone. She had a momentary impulse to turn and flee back down the wharf to try and get aboard the boat. But as she turned and saw the lights of the side-wheeler slide away into the darkness she realized it was too late even for that. With troubled eyes she watched its ghostly shape go off in the distance.

She turned to try and seek assistance from someone only

to find herself face to face with a handsome man in a caped coat. She had almost bumped into him and she quickly apologized, "I'm sorry!"

"As much my fault as yours," the man said in a pleasant, cultured voice.

"I wasn't looking where I was going," she said. "I expected to be met by somebody. It's rather frightening that they haven't turned up."

The gaunt, handsome face showed a sympathetic smile. "May I be of any help? I'm a visitor here for a few weeks. My name is Barnabas Collins."

Lara stared at him. "Barnabas Collins!" she repeated. "Then you must know Quentin Collins. He's the one supposed to meet me."

"Indeed?" He lifted his heavy black brows in mild astonishment. "Quentin is my cousin. It's strange he's not here as he promised."

"Could he be ill?" she wondered. "He mentioned not being well in his letters."

The man nodded. "That must be it," he said. "I know he hasn't been quite himself lately. That would explain his not being here. But you mustn't worry. I can see you safely back to the estate. You can spend the night as my guest in the old house where I'm staying and in the morning go to Collinwood. The houses are close together." Lara hesitated. After all, she didn't know this man. It was too upsetting. She was bewildered by the mention of two houses. When Quentin had written her he'd given her the idea that there was only one large house on the estate.

She said, "Surely there must be some other way. I could go to a hotel. I don't want to be a nuisance to you."

Smiling ironically, he said, "I fear our local hotel is not suitable for a young woman of your breeding. And since I'm living on Quentin's estate and in the original house built there long before Collinwood you're quite welcome. Quentin would be upset to find out I let you go elsewhere."

She listened and still hesitated to accept his offer. The wharf was occupied only by the workers rolling up hogsheads and carrying up crates of other goods that had come on the vessel. Soon they would have their tasks completed and there would be no one. Barnabas' handsome face was highlighted by the flickering flame of a nearby torch as he studied her.

She said, "My name is Lara Balfour. Quentin Collins and my father were friends."

"Of course!" Barnabas said. "You are the composer's daughter. Quentin has spoken to me of both you and your father. And I have heard the record of that lovely waltz on Quentin's marvelous new gramophone."

She managed a wan smile, feeling she should be grateful to the pleasant man for his offer and accept it. After all, he was Quentin's cousin. And, as he'd explained, she could move across to the main house in the morning.

"If I may impose on you," she said, "you'll find my luggage on the wharf."

Barnabas bowed. "I'll call my man, Benson, and have him look after your things."

He turned and waved to a short, stout man who had been standing a little distance away. Now the man came hurrying forward. He wore a bowler hat and had a round, pleasant face. Lara at once decided he was someone she would like.

Barnabas explained, "This is Miss Lara Balfour, Benson. She has come here to be a guest of my cousin Quentin. Since he's not here to meet her, I'm taking her to the old house where she can be our guest for the night."

The little man bowed politely to her and with a startled look on his good-natured face asked his master, "She will stay the night in the old house?"

Barnabas nodded. "It will be all right, Benson. You can take her to my cousin in the morning."

"Yes, sir. Just as you say, sir."

"Her luggage is on the wharf. Get one of the workers to help you carry it to our carriage. Then we'll drive back to Collinwood." He turned to Lara again as the servant went down the wharf to locate her things. "I'm here to do some serious writing of a book on botanical specimens of the area. Benson is not used to my having guests."

"I still feel that I'm intruding."

"Not at all," Barnabas said warmly. "I'm most interested in meeting you. I don't see too much of Cousin Quentin these days. I'm busy and he's not been too well. And he has the fishing business to supervise. So it's possible we might not have met at all except for this chance encounter. I'm grateful for it."

Lara listened to him vaguely as her attention had been caught by two of the dock workers who had taken a stand a few feet away from where she and Barnabas were talking and were staring at them. Next the two whispered to each other in a furtive manner. One of them shook his head, as if in disbelief, and then they walked off into the darkness.

She had the eerie sensation that the brief discussion and amazement of the two had been based on seeing her there with Barnabas Collins. But why? He seemed nice enough. And he apparently hadn't taken any notice of them at all. Still, a tiny nerve of fear stirred in her again.

Lara shivered. To cover her uneasiness, she said, "This drizzle is cold for June. I feel chilled."

"We'll make you a good fire and give you some wine when we get to the house," Barnabas promised her. Taking her by the arm, he led her from the wharf up the steep street to a waiting carriage with a lantern mounted by the driver's seat. "I'm sorry it's an open carriage," he said, as he helped her up into it.

The hand he gave her was icy cold. She'd never felt a hand so cold, except that of her father when he was resting in his casket. The thought had come to her automatically and she was startled by it. She began to think she'd exaggerated the coldness of his hand because of her nerves.

Settling back in the carriage seat, she said, "I'll manage very well in this. I'm so lucky to be getting a drive to Collinwood."

Barnabas sat beside her, his hands resting on his cane. It was black with a silver head shaped like a wolf's. The carriage vibrated slightly as Benson and another man placed her luggage in the back.

She apologized, "I have a good many things with me. I planned to remain the summer."

"I'm sure Quentin will insist that you do," Barnabas assured her. "When the weather is pleasant this is a truly lovely spot."

"So he said," she agreed. "It has been in your family for many years. I mean the estate of Collinwood."

"Yes, the town of Collinsport is named after our family. We came here first in the late seventeen-hundreds. A lot of us have lived and died since then."

A strange, haunted quality in the way he spoke made her stare at him. He had a heavy head of black hair, some of which tumbled carelessly across his high forehead; his eyebrows were darkly prominent and his eyes deep-set and piercing. Strong lines showed at either side of his mouth. His lips were rather thick and when he smiled powerful white teeth were revealed. All in all, he was strikingly good-looking if you discounted his sallow skin and the suggestion of gauntness about him.

She said, "You do not live here all the time?"

"I merely return for visits."

Benson had taken his seat at the front and now he urged the horses into motion. The wheels of the carriage creaked as they moved up the narrow street in the wet darkness. Lara gathered her cloak about her and trembled both from cold and nerves.

"It's a quaint old village," she observed as she studied the weathered one-story shops they were passing.

"We're rather isolated here," he said quietly. "Progress is slow to find us. While Collinwood is a fine house with most modern conveniences, you'll discover the countryside around is fairly primitive."

She managed a small smile. "It's different from anything I've known. I'm sure I'm going to enjoy it."

"I hope so," he said. "You will hear many legends about Collinwood. The fishermen are a superstitious lot who see a ghost in every shadow."

She gazed at his strong profile. "Are there supposed to be ghosts at Collinwood?"

"We're said to have our fair share," he agreed rather bitterly. "But I doubt if they'll ever bother you."

"I also doubt it," she said. "I've never had any experience with the supernatural."

"Indeed," Barnabas Collins observed with interest.

"I've really had very little contact with death aside from my father's recent passing," she went on. "And since then I have been wondering. I mean, if there is another world."

"Very natural."

She frowned a little. "Do you think that people can return after death?"

"It's an interesting possibility."

"But do you have a personal opinion?"

His handsome face showed a wise smile. "Like most anyone you may ask, I fear my opinion would be biased."

She agreed thoughtfully. "I suppose you're right. We're all entitled to our personal views on the subject."

"Exactly."

"And who can tell if any of us are right?"

"Who can tell?" he echoed.

They had left the narrow main street now and were driving along a wooded road such as she'd rarely seen in her days of living in Philadelphia and the surrounding country. As Barnabas had said, this was a bleak, isolated place. Nowhere did she see a house.

"Not many people live along here," she ventured.

"No," he said. "My family owns all the land adjacent to this road and they haven't encouraged building along here. The Collins family have a strong desire for privacy."

"I see." She wondered if she'd made a bad error. Surely she'd get very bored in this quiet corner of Maine. She'd had no idea it was so grim and deserted.

Benson urged the horses forward and the lantern by his seat swayed with the motion of the groaning wheels, eerily lighting up the night for a short way. To Lara the drive seemed endless, though she guessed it was actually not all that far. She was about to speak to Barnabas again when suddenly the little man driving brought the carriage to a jerking halt. The unexpected stopping nearly pitched her forward, but Barnabas had grasped her with a restraining hand. She was going to ask what was wrong when she saw all too clearly.

Standing directly in the road, blocking their way, was a snarling wolf-like creature clearly visible in the glow of the lantern. Benson tried to calm the horses as they reared and neighed. The bristling animal looked yellow-green, its eyes were catlike, glowing in the reflected lamplight. Its mouth was open and slavering, revealing ugly white fangs. And as Lara stared in horror it gave a blood-curdling howl!

Barnabas stood up in the carriage. "Drive on!" he ordered Benson. "It will give way. If you hold the horses back, they'll really panic!"

""Yes, sir!" the little man gasped and raised his whip to the horses.

The creature in the road gave another menacing howl and then ran off into the woods as the horses plunged forward. The carriage swayed as the horses raced on wildly. Lara held onto the side of the carriage and again Barnabas came to her assistance by placing an arm around her.

After a few moments they left the woods behind them for open fields and the ocean on her side of the road. She lay back against the seat as the horses slowed down and came under firm control. She gave the man beside her a frightened glance.

"What was that?"

"A kind of wild dog," Barnabas Collins said. "Quentin's brother Conrad has a kennel out by the barns where he raises a crossbreed. Every now and then one of them escapes and roams the countryside.

"I was sure, it was a wolf," she gasped.

Barnabas glanced at her. "I doubt that we have any wolves left in this part of the country."

"It looked like any picture I've seen of one."

He shrugged. "You could be right," he said quietly. And then he surprised her by adding, "If I were you I wouldn't mention this to Quentin when you meet him tomorrow."

"Why not?"

Barnabas hesitated. "It could cause trouble between him and Conrad. He doesn't get on well with his younger brother and they're always quarreling about Conrad having the dogs."

"I see," she said, aware that this bad feeling between the two brothers was to be another hazard of her stay at Collinwood.

Barnabas must have read her thoughts for he quickly said, "It's not anything for you to be concerned about. They get on well most of the time, but I felt I should explain."

She nodded, thankful for his concern. "I appreciate it."

Barnabas indicated a great, square dark mansion ahead and to the left, a sprawling big house overlooking the cliffs and the ocean. It had a fantastic array of tall chimneys and at the moment its windows showed no lights at all. "That is the new Collinwood where you'll be a guest."

They were driving by it. Even in the mist she could study it. "I find it very imposing."

He smiled grimly. "A good deal of our history is tied up in that house and in the older one I'm taking you to. In the hallway of Collinwood there is a portrait of the first Barnabas Collins."

"I must look for it."

"You'll not have any difficulty noticing it," he predicted ."I'm told he and I bear a strange resemblance to one another."

They drove past the big house and then by some outbuildings. At last they came to a smaller stone house and Benson brought the horses to a halt. Barnabas got out of the carriage and assisted her to the ground. Once more their hands touched and she was conscious of that weird icy coldness of his flesh. He was leading her to the entrance of the dark old house when from close by that blood-curdling banshee howl came again to freeze her with terror!

CHAPTER 2

For a moment her sudden terror rooted her to the spot. Then Barnabas urged her up the worn stone steps of the old house with a mild, "You mustn't let those cries alarm you. Conrad's kennels are not far from here. We are used to such sounds in the night."

"I'm sorry," she murmured.

At the top of the steps he opened the heavy oak door and waited for her to enter a shadowed hallway. She was still uneasy as to whether she had made the right decision. But what other course had been open to her?

Barnabas showed her down the high-ceilinged hall to the double doors leading into an elegant living room furnished with priceless antiques. Ornate chairs and divans filled the room and candles flickered in silver candlesticks set out on the mantle of the marble fireplace and on several of the tables. A log fire blazed in the fireplace casting a rosy, romantic glow over it all.

Some of her tension left her and she turned to Barnabas Collins with a delighted smile. "This is a wonderful old room!"

He looked pleased. "I'm tremendously fond of it," he said. "The house is largely unused now, but whenever I come back I ask to be allowed to stay here. You will find Collinwood much larger and equally well appointed."

She gazed at the gaunt, handsome face of the man who had

befriended her and wondered what there was about him that set him apart from most men she'd met. He had a certain air, an aloofness, and yet he was pleasant enough. She couldn't quite comprehend it.

His eyes were fixed on her and she was aware of a certain sadness in them, a sadness she couldn't understand. Rather awkwardly, she said, "Collinwood must be magnificent to overshadow this house. I'm sure you and your wife are bound to be very happy here."

"I have no wife," he said. "Benson takes care of the house for me. He is extremely competent. As soon as he brings in your luggage I'll have him get you some food and drink. Then he'll prepare a room for you."

"Please don't go to any trouble."

"It's no bother," he assured her. "We have plenty of room for guests. However, because of my peculiar working schedule we seldom have them."

Lara moved across the room, taking note of the fine china, silver and pottery set out on the tables and sideboard. She suddenly found herself studying an exquisitely carved piece of marble in the shape of a delicate hand. Touching it with her fingers she turned to the man in the caped coat.

"This is so unusual!"

"Yes," he said with one of his occasional grim smiles. "I came across that in Florence and brought it back with me. It was part of a fine example of gravestone decoration which had been destroyed by vandals. I salvaged the hand from the debris and kept it. I believe it to be the exact replica of the hand of the young woman whose grave it once graced."

There was something in the way he so casually spoke of the graveyard that sent a tiny chill through her. She stared at the hand again. "It has a strange history."

"I find old graveyards fascinating," he said quietly.

She looked at him. "I haven't given the matter much consideration," she admitted. "I suppose I've always thought of them as rather grim, sad places. Probably I've avoided them. My mother died when I was very young. And my father disliked talking about death. But I was in a graveyard a few months ago when I buried him."

"I'm sorry," Barnabas Collins apologized. "It was tactless of me to bring the subject up."

"No, it's all right," she said at once. "And in any case you are probably right. A great deal of history and the romance of the past can be discovered in our burial places."

The deep-set eyes of Barnabas Collins burned into her. "Your comment shows intellect," he said. "I have been criticized in some quarters because I spend a great deal of time visiting the local graveyards and making myself familiar with them. Some of the villagers regard my behavior as odd."

"That is very wrong of them."

"Yes, I think so. I have an idea my actions disturb Quentin as well. My cousin does not take much interest in the family history. He is more absorbed with the present and the future."

Lara smiled. "Well, people shouldn't all think alike."

"Nor do they," he assured her.

At that moment Benson entered the room with a tray containing bread, cheese and a tall bottle of red wine. The little man set these on a table near her. "I hope this is to your taste, miss."

She offered him a look of gratitude. "You're being much too kind."

Benson's round face radiated pleasure. He turned to Barnabas and said, "I plan to open the large bedroom at the head of the stairway for the young lady. Will that be satisfactory, sir?"

"I'd say so," Barnabas said. "It is on the end of the house away from the kennels and their unsettling sounds. Be sure the room is not damp. Better light a few logs in the fireplace at once and have the place comfortable."

As the servant hurried off she smiled at Barnabas. "I'm keeping you from your bed. It's getting very late."

The man in the caped coat stood by the fireplace watching her. The changing glow of the flames reflected on his strong face, giving it a romantic appeal.

"I am a night person," he said. "I seldom sleep until the dawn."

"You are unusual."

He shrugged. "It has become part of my pattern of existence. The night has appeal for me. I prefer to work during these hours because of the privacy and silence they offer. I sleep a good part of the day."

"I see," she said. "Will you share some of this food and wine with me?"

"No. I rarely eat or drink at this hour."

She sipped some of the excellent wine. "I feel selfish enjoying this alone."

"It was prepared for you," he said, staring at her with those deep-set eyes. "May I ask if you and my cousin Quentin are very close friends?"

"We've never met," she said. "I know him only through his writing letters to my father. That is why I hesitated to accept his invitation to holiday here. But he finally persuaded me."

"I thought it was something like that," Barnabas said, still studying her closely. "I trust you will enjoy your stay here. I'm sure Quentin will be a charming host. He can be if he likes. And you mustn't hold his not being on hand to meet you tonight against him.

He undoubtedly will have a good excuse."

"I'm sure of that."

Barnabas frowned slightly. "However, on the chance things do not turn out as you'd like, please don't hesitate to get in touch with me."

She was slightly surprised. "I'll remember that."

"You can always leave a message here with Benson. And when I see him in the evening he'll give it to me. I'd like you to feel I'm someone you can depend on."

"You've done too much already!"

"Not at all. Collinwood is a strange place in many ways, as I have warned you. You may have some trouble adapting to it. And I'd like to be of help."

"You have been."

As she finished her snack his words troubled her. Part of the mystery about him was his manner of hinting that Collinwood was not the simple country house she expected, that she would find things here that she might not understand and which would disturb her. She wished that she knew him better so she might query him more frankly. But she realized she couldn't.

"I'm ready for sleep now," she admitted with a small smile as she rose from the tray.

"Come with me," Barnabas said. "Benson will have your room ready by this time."

They mounted a short flight of stairs and the door to the bedroom reserved for her was open. A welcome rosy tint flooded the room from the blazing fire in the big fireplace. Benson had turned down the sheets of the ancient fourposter. All was in readiness for her.

Barnabas said, "I trust you will sleep well."

"I'm sure I shall." She smiled at him. "Thank you again."

"Goodnight," he said. "Benson will see you safely across to Collinwood in the morning."

"I'll tell your cousin of your great kindness to me."

He looked grimly amused. "I wouldn't dwell on it. He is rather touchy, and it could annoy him. But do remember not to mention that wild creature we encountered on the road."

She gave a tiny shudder at the vision of the snarling thing. "I'll not say anything about it."

"It will be to your advantage not to." He took her hand again as he said, "Goodnight."

Lara closed the door after him and bolted it. Once again she'd been shocked by the strange coldness of his hand. He surely must be the victim of some circulatory disorder!

She prepared for bed, filled with troubling thoughts of what sort of man Quentin Collins would turn out to be. Surely he'd let her down tonight but Barnabas had hinted there could be a good reason for that. And then there was the problem of Quentin's brother. This Conrad must be a strange person to breed such vicious wolf-like animals as the one she'd seen an hour ago. It could not be too safe to walk about the estate alone with such creatures liable to be stalking you. No wonder Quentin and his brother were continually at odds about Conrad's strange obsession.

She would keep silent, as she had promised, about the snarling animal she'd seen. But when the first opportunity presented itself she would try to learn more about the kennels. No doubt she'd have a chance to question Conrad directly. With this thought she closed her eyes and sought sleep.

Her quiet home in Philadelphia seemed very far away. Had she been indiscreet in accepting the invitation of a young man she'd never actually met? But then his letters had been so sincere and engaging, and she had been so lonely after her father's death. And this cousin of his, Barnabas, was a tremendously interesting person, though she still had the feeling she didn't understand him. She smiled to herself in the darkness. Why should she be able to understand him? She'd led such a sheltered life that she had really never known any men aside from her father. But this summer would change things, she promised herself. There would be three men to get to know – Quentin, Conrad, and Barnabas. Telling herself that her father would be pleased at her little adventure into the world, she drifted off to sleep.

What wakened her was a soft beating against the shuttered windows of her room. At first she sleepily tried to ignore the sound. But it persisted along with a kind of sort, impatient mewling. She opened her eyes with a frown wrinkling her lovely forehead and stared up into the near darkness of the room. Faintly glowing embers in the fireplace opposite the foot of her bed kept the place from being pitch-dark. And suddenly there was Barnabas standing by the side of her bed wearing his caped coat just as when he'd said goodnight. He was gazing at her with a sad intensity. His burning eyes met hers hypnotically. She could not move or speak.

And yet she was not actually frightened. She was caught up in a kind of eerie spell. The handsome man with the rumpled black hair and gaunt features took a step nearer her and then bent down. His lips touched her throat and she could feel that they were as icy cold as his hands had been. Yet she was still unable to move or utter a protest. Then she experienced a new sensation, a burning at her throat in the midst of the chill of his kiss. It was almost painful, and she felt a weakness surge through her as if all consciousness was draining away, and yet the experience was pleasant!

Then she blacked out. She had no further recollection of the episode or any dreams to mar her sleep. But when she opened her eyes to the streaks of daylight showing in through the shutters, she recalled

Barnabas standing by her bed and that odd kiss on the throat. But in the bright reality of the day the episode seemed nightmarish.

Throwing aside the bedclothes, she put on her slippers and a robe to make her way to the door and test the bolt she'd so securely fixed in place the night before. It was there just as she'd left it. Then he couldn't have been in her room. It had all been a bad dream. No matter how vivid it seemed, it could not have really happened. She stood there uncertainly, conscious of a tingling feeling at her throat. She touched the spot with her fingers and then went over to the dresser mirror to study herself.

There was a barely noticeable red mark on her throat. Staring at it, she felt this offered a simple explanation of her nightmare. She'd been bitten by some mosquito or other insect and the annoyance of the bite had triggered off the weird dream. Satisfied, she began to dress.

When she left her room to go downstairs she found the old house oddly dark and quiet. There wasn't a sound. The steps creaking under her as she slowly descended them sounded loud beyond any reason. Almost the minute she reached the lower hallway the diminutive Benson popped into view with his usual friendly air. "Breakfast is waiting in the dining room, miss."

Lara felt sure the huge, gloomy dining room had not been used in some time and she could not help but wonder where Barnabas took his meals. As Benson hovered over the table with a silver coffee pot, she asked, "Does Mr. Barnabas Collins eat here?"

The little man seemed embarrassed. He hesitated in pouring her coffee to state, "No, miss. I take him whatever he requires to his room in the cellar."

This came as a surprise to her. With all this large house at his disposal, Barnabas preferred to work in the dark shadows of the cellar. "Why does he work down there?"

The little man was evasive. "I suppose you might call it a matter of taste, miss. He prefers the quiet and the seclusion the cellar offers."

"I find it quiet enough up here."

"Yes, miss." He finished pouring her coffee and left the room quickly.

She could see that this was to be another unanswered question in a house containing so many odd enigmas. In spite of the hospitality Barnabas had shown her, she suddenly found the old house depressing. She hurried through the rest of her breakfast and when Benson reappeared told him she was ready to leave.

The short walk to Collinwood was a revelation. Benson accompanied her, explaining he would arrange with the handyman at Collinwood to have her luggage sent over after her. In daylight the estate was an imposing one. Even the old brick house in which she'd spent the night took on a noble look when one could see its ivy-clad walls.

As for Collinwood, it was truly impressive. It looked even larger than it had glimpsed through the trysts of the previous night. There were a number of barns to the rear of it and the mansion faced directly toward the cliff and the ocean beyond. The view of the water was magnificent and the lawns and hedges were neat and well kept. Benson kept up a polite running conversation explaining about the estate as they walked.

Waving toward a point along the cliffs to the right, he said, "Over there is Widows' Hill. Quite a fantastic story told about that. But of course you'll hear all about it from Mr. Quentin. The family cemetery is beyond the old house at the bottom of a field. All the generations of the Collins family have been buried there."

She gave the little man a knowing look. "I'd imagine that would be a favorite place of Mr. Barnabas."

Benson showed surprise. "As it happens, he does go down there often."

"I assumed he would. He explained his deep interest in cemeteries to me last night."

It seemed to her a relieved look crossed the servant's round face. "Ah, yes," he agreed. "Mr. Barnabas is fond of graveyards and the like."

They reached the entrance to the commanding mansion and the servant lifted the heavy brass door knocker to announce their presence. Then he stood by with a slightly nervous air. Lara had the thought that he was not enjoying this task Barnabas had left him. It seemed an endless time before the door opened to reveal a beautiful, dark-haired young woman standing there, surprise on her pleasant though somewhat sullen face. She had large gray eyes which were wide open and staring now. "Yes?" she inquired in a low, husky voice.

"Begging your pardon, Miss Edmonds," the little man apologized. "This is Miss Lara Balfour. I believe she is to be a guest of Mr. Quentin's. He wasn't at the wharf to meet her last night so my master gave her a room in the old house."

The girl was still staring at her in astonishment. She said, "I'll let Quentin know you are here, Miss Balfour. I'm sure he didn't expect you."

It was Lara's turn to be startled. "But the date was arranged clearly in his letter."

The dark girl said, "He'd best explain to you himself. He's in his study. I'll take you to him. My name is Catherine Edmonds. I take care of Quentin's great-aunt."

"He wrote me about you," Lara said.

Benson looked upset. "Shall I send the young lady's bags over. Miss Edmonds?"

The girl seemed annoyed. "Yes, I suppose you'd better."

Benson offered them both a polite bow and hurried off in the direction of the old house. Catherine Edmonds took Lara inside. The main hallway was large and truly imposing. And high on one of the walls was the portrait Barnabas Collins had mentioned – the portrait of the first Barnabas, who indeed had the same features as the man she'd met. She was given no time to study the portrait in detail as Catherine guided her down a dim corridor to the study.

The door was closed. Catherine knocked on it and a moment later it was opened by a youngish man of proud, sensitive features, wearing black side-whiskers to match his thick head of black hair. His eyebrows arched delicately over wide-spaced, piercing eyes. He wore a dark gray suit with a golden watch chain showing across his vest and a stiff collar with neat open points ornamented by a light gray cravat. He stared at them in consternation.

"Yes?"

Catherine Edmonds gave him a look of reproach. "This is Lara Balfour. She arrived last night and was the guest of Barnabas at the old house. Apparently she didn't receive your last letter."

The young man had gone very pale. "Apparently not." He offered Lara a troubled smile. "Welcome to Collinwood, Miss Balfour. I'm Quentin Collins."

She took his proffered hand. "I feel that I'm intruding," she said. "Did you send me a message I didn't receive?"

"Please don't worry about it," Quentin Collins said hastily. Turning to Catherine, he told her, "Go prepare a room for Miss Balfour. I'll have a chat with her and explain the situation here."

Catherine gave her a bleak glance. Then she asked Quentin, "On the third floor?"

"I suppose so," he said impatiently. "Whatever you think will be best." He stood back for Lara to enter the study. "Please come in, Miss Balfour."

She gave him a worried smile. "I had no intention of disturbing you. And please call me by my first name, as you have been doing in your letters. 'Miss Balfour' sounds entirely too formal between friends."

He smiled. "Very well. You shall be Lara and I shall be Quentin." He pulled out a chair for her.

She sat in the easy chair and studied the book-lined walls of the study. It was a good-sized room with a fireplace and a large desk before which young Quentin Collins now stood. She noticed how pale he was and recalled his references to poor health in his letters. She was also upset to have heard there had been a last letter which must have arrived in Philadelphia after she'd left.

"It appears you didn't expect me last night."

He stood with his hands clasped behind his back. "To be

honest, Lara, I didn't. Though now that you're here, I'm glad you came. I mailed you a letter advising you that my health was so much worse I didn't think it wise for you to visit me at this time. Of course you didn't get it."

"No."

"I'm happy it's worked out this way, since I'm really feeling much better," Quentin went on with a smile. "We'll go through with our plans as we made them. You shall be our guest for the summer."

"Not if you're ill," she protested.

"I've been much better since I sent you the letter," Quentin said earnestly. "The seizures from which I've suffered have troubled me a great deal less lately."

"I still feel that I should leave."

"Not at all. I can only apologize that I wasn't at the wharf to meet you last night. Of course I supposed you'd gotten the letter."

"I managed very well," she said. "Your cousin, Barnabas, was most kind to me."

Quentin frowned. "So Barnabas was there."

"Yes. And when I explained my plight he was most helpful. I stayed the night as his guest at the old house."

"Indeed," Quentin said, his wide-set eyes fixed on her keenly. "My cousin is rather an odd fellow. I'm happy that you found him in such a good mood."

Lara was surprised by this remark. "He seemed very nice."

"Did you see him this morning before you left?" There was almost a note of sarcasm in the question.

"As a matter of fact, no. I believe he was at work in his rooms in the cellar."

"Undoubtedly," Quentin said with what might have been construed as a thin sneer. "Barnabas is seen very rarely, if at all, during the daylight hours."

"He must be a person of remarkable dedication to his work."

"Yes," Quentin said without enthusiasm. "Before dinner tonight I must play you my record of your father's lovely waltz. I have our gramophone in the living room."

"Thank you," she said. "I've never heard the record. My father was against mechanical music machines. But then you know that."

Quentin smiled sadly. "Yes. We had that discussion in our letters. I felt very bad about his death. That is why I initially thought it would be a fine idea to have you visit here."

"You made it sound very attractive. And it is a lovely place."

"With some drawbacks," he was willing to admit. "Still, Collinwood is one of the fine estates in this part of Maine. We are isolated but we do enjoy our privacy because of it."

"Barnabas mentioned your brother."

He nodded. "You'll meet Conrad this evening. He is an outdoor man and I allow him to supervise the tenant farmers. And of course he has his kennels to occupy him as well. Did Barnabas mention that my brother raised dogs?"

"I think perhaps he did," she said diplomatically, recalling the warning Barnabas had given her not to stress the dogs.

Quentin sighed. "I think he gives too much time to his hobby but I'm unable to stop him. And then the breed he raises is a wild, mixed strain popular only with him."

The conversation was interrupted by the return of Catherine Edmonds. She told Quentin. "I have the room ready."

"Excellent." He turned to Lara. "I'm sure you'll want to rest. Catherine will show you upstairs."

Lara rose. "Please remember I'm willing to leave at any time. If you feel unwell again don't hesitate to tell me."

"I'm going to be better just because you're here, Lara," he said warmly. "I do feel that." And he saw her out to the corridor.

Catherine walked stiffly up the stairs ahead of her without turning or saying a word to her on the way. Not until she showed her into the large bedroom on the third floor did she break the silence between them.

"This will be yours," she said rather coldly. "It has a view of the ocean."

Lara walked over to the large window and pulled back the blue drapes which matched the blue and white decor of the bedroom. She wanted to be friendly with this girl who was about her own age, but she could tell that Catherine resented her. She deeply regretted she'd not received that last letter and so avoided this unhappy plight.

Staring out at the ocean for a moment, she turned and commented, "It is lovely from this window. Collinwood has a fine location."

Catherine Edmonds was staring directly at her. "You plan to stay?"

"Quentin seems anxious that I should," she said awkwardly. "I don't suppose I've really decided."

"This is not a happy place."

Lara was surprised by this bald statement. "You're referring to Quentin's illness," she suggested. "But he told me he's feeling much better."

"You'll find out."

Lara was feeling increasingly uneasy. "I'd like us to be friends."

Catherine's smile was cold. "Your things will be here from the old house shortly."

"Thank you."

The other girl's eyes suddenly fixed on her throat. "Did you know you have a red mark on your throat?"

She reached up to it defensively. "It's nothing. I know about it."

"I wondered," Catherine said, in almost a mocking tone. And then she added, "I'll see your luggage is sent up as soon as it gets here." And she went out.

Lara stared after her. Quite plainly this girl was not happy to see her. She resented her coming to the house. And there could only be one reason, Lara concluded. Catherine was in love with Quentin and feared losing him to her. It had to be that. Lara thought Quentin was a widower. There had been a vague reference to this in one of his letters to her father. She tried unsuccessfully to recall what had been written.

The room she had been given was large, but not as luxuriously furnished as the rest of the house. Trust Catherine not to give her the best. There was a good-sized bed with a table beside it, a matching dresser, some easy chairs and braided circular rugs on the hard floors. The room was apparently lighted by a lamp hanging from a center ceiling fixture. There were doors in addition to the one leading to the hall and she supposed these belonged to closets.

She opened one of the doors and found a big, dark closet. She stepped inside to determine if there were hooks on the rear wall of it. As she moved into the shadows she suddenly was terrified to hear the sound of gasping breathing from directly behind her. And in the next instant, bony fingers grasped her arm!

CHAPTER 3

Lara screamed as the bony fingers tightened about her arm. And then there came a crackle of crazed laughter in her ear and a wheezy voice informed her, "Sang a dog with a pointed muzzle and by his spells a wolf created!" The weird incantation convinced Lara that she was dealing with a human, not a ghost. Regaining a small measure of courage, she turned to see the crouched figure dimly outlined in the shadows. She had a glimpse of scraggly long hair streaming down from a pinched face with a hooked nose. It was the figure of an old woman. An old woman wearing some loose, formless dress.

Lara finally wrenched her arm free of the ancient hag's grip and took a step back from her. "Who are you and what do you want?"

The old woman chuckled again and lifted a thin forefinger slyly. "I call thee evil spirit, cruel spirit, merciless spirit. Bad spirit who sittest in the cemetery and comes to place a knot in Erica's tongue!"

She edged out of the dark closet as she listened to the mad old woman in fascination. At the mention of the name Erica she guessed at once that this must be the great-aunt Quentin had spoken of, the old woman whom Catherine Edmonds was responsible for. Erica Collins, nearly a century old and senile!

"What's happening here?" It was Quentin Collins who called out this question as he came striding into her room.

Lara escaped from the closet to hurry to him. "I'm sorry I made such a fuss. I had a scare."

Instantly the unkempt, scarecrow figure of Erica Collins came sidling out of the closet with a cunning grin on her emaciated face.

Quentin studied her in anger. "So it was you, Aunt Erica!" And he turned to Lara apologetically. "She is supposed to be confined to her own apartment on this floor. I can't imagine how she escaped."

"It's all right," Laura said weakly.

"Catherine should have found you a room on the floor below," the young man raged. He turned to the elderly woman, who stood crouched against the wall near the closet door. "Aunt Erica, you must go back to your own room."

The old woman looked as if she might burst into tears. "It's a pestilent disease, nephew; they call it lycanthropy!" At that moment Catherine Edmonds appeared. She gave Lara a mocking glance and went directly over to the old woman and took her by a skinny arm.

"Come along, Aunt Erica," she said in a soothing tone. "There may be visitors waiting for you in the apartment and you won't be there to greet them."

The old woman chuckled at this and allowed Catherine to lead her out of the room. Quentin watched the two go, disgust written on his sensitive face.

"Please try to forget this distressing incident. Aunt Erica is completely mad. Catherine is supposed to see she doesn't roam about the house. I'll have a few words with her about this."

"Please! Not on my account. I understand."

Quentin still looked grim. "Aunt Erica was always a strange sort of woman. Now that she's nearly a hundred she's a problem. Most of her time she's confined to her bed but occasionally she wanders as she did just now."

"It was only that I wasn't expecting her," Lara said. "I'll know another time."

"There shouldn't be another time."

With further apologies he left her. Only then did she have a chance to think about the old woman's words and wonder what they meant. Probably nothing, she decided, yet it had been extremely unpleasant. She hoped she wouldn't have an experience like it again.

A male servant brought up her luggage about twenty minutes later and she occupied herself unpacking and worrying whether she was making a mistake or not. Perhaps she should have insisted on taking the first boat back to Boston. Then she thought about Barnabas and his promise of friendship and help. It seemed to her she should discuss it all with him before she made up her mind. She had liked Quentin's handsome cousin and looked forward to another meeting with him.

Oddly, Quentin seemed very cold towards Barnabas. She could feel the resentment the young master of Collinwood felt for his cousin.

And she wondered why this strained relationship between them should exist.

With her unpacking finished and luncheon behind her, Lara decided to take a walk in the gardens. It was a lovely June day and yet cool enough to be enjoyable. The gardens were in full bloom and she finally sat down on a marble bench set out along one of the gravel walks. From there she could stare out across the calm, silver waters of the ocean.

She heard a footstep on the gravel and looked up to see Catherine standing there studying her with one of those mocking smiles. Catherine asked, "How do you feel about Aunt Erica?"

Lara wasn't going to give the other girl anything to gloat about. Very calmly, she said, "She's a poor mad old creature. She'll not frighten me again."

The large gray eyes of the dark girl held a taunting gleam. "She plans to place a spell on you."

"A spell?" Lara wasn't prepared for anything like this.

Catherine nodded. "Yes. She considers herself a witch, you know."

"I pity her insanity."

"Don't be too sure it's all insanity." Catherine said slyly. "When she was younger, Erica was the leader of a group of practitioners of black magic in the Collinsport area. She learned a great deal from the native servants who came here from the West Indies on the clipper ships. The villagers claim she mastered voodoo rituals and could transform herself into other creatures. They still whisper about her evil powers."

"A mad old woman. And that is all."

"Believe what you like," Catherine told her. "I'm warning you of what she was. Even in her madness she has moments of startling clarity – and she resents you coming here."

"You probably instilled that idea in her poor muddled brain."

The other girl crimsoned. "I didn't need to. She hated you at first sight. She claims she has a wicked curse on you."

"Thank you for the information," Lara said. "I have an idea who resents my coming here most. And why."

Catherine looked upset. "My thanks for trying to give you good advice." She wheeled about and hurried back toward the house.

The exchange left Lara bothered. She wished that she could go straight to Barnabas at this moment and get his ideas, but that was impossible. So she got up from the bench and walked out toward the barns. She hadn't gone far when she heard the clamor from the kennels. Her approach was the signal for wild barking from the dogs kept by Quentin's brother.

The large run behind the kennels contained at least a half dozen huge, ferocious-looking grayish animals who bounded against the high picket fence confining them and barked at her. She stood a foot or so from the fence and tried to identify the animal they'd met in the road the night before. There was none to match the hulking threat of that nocturnal creature.

She was standing there listening to the snarling of the big dogs with a sort of fascination when a tall, young man limped over to join her. With a quizzical smile on a face so much like Quentin's she knew they had to be brothers, he said, "You find my dogs interesting?"

Lara turned to him with a smile. "I'm frightened of them but they do intrigue me. You must be Conrad Collins."

"I am," he said. This younger brother of Quentin's seemed good-natured enough. He was a few inches taller than Quentin and had a small mustache. He dressed in rough outdoor clothing which made him seem more the farmhand than a gentleman farmer. And most noticeable of all was his clubfoot which gave him his limp.

She said, "I've been looking forward to meeting you."

"And I've just been told about your arrival," he said with a look of quiet amusement. "You're Lara Balfour, whose father wrote Quentin's waltz."

"You know about it."

"I hardly have any choice since Quentin plays it on his new gramophone nearly every night," the young man said with mock ruefulness. "I'm beginning to wish he had some other favorite tune."

"I've never heard the record," she confessed.

"You will," he promised. "I understood your visit here had been postponed. I'm glad you didn't change your plans; the place needs a new face."

She laughed. "The only thing that prevented me from postponing my visit was the fact I didn't get your brother's last letter."

The tall young man shrugged. "Just as well. Quentin is a person of whims, and much of his illness is imaginary. Your being here should be a tonic to us all."

The big dogs had continued their bounding against the fence and their furious barking. Conrad limped over to the fence and spoke to them sharply. The almost instant result was a calming down of the huge animals. Reluctantly, with low, ominous growls, they slunk back. He turned to her apologetically.

"They aren't always like this," he said. "A stranger excites them."

"Wouldn't they be dangerous if they escaped? Why do you breed such savage beasts?"

He limped back to stand beside her, a shadow of displeasure on his sensitive face. "I like their strength and courage. You don't find it often among humans."

She stared at him. "Then you really train them to be like they are?"

He smiled grimly. "It's part their natural instinct and part my training. My pride is that I've developed a unique strain of animal."

"I'm sure you have," she said. "Aren't your neighbors afraid of them? On the loose they could be killers."

"I disagree," Conrad said in a curt voice. "They are trained to harm no one unless conditions call for it. They are taught to guard against intruders and defend their master. That is all."

It was her turn to offer him a rueful smile. "I only hope they understand that clearly."

"They are much smarter than most people can imagine."

She was about to mention the unhappy experience of the previous night when the snarling, wolflike animal had frightened the horses. But if Barnabas had warned her not to mention it to Quentin, perhaps it would be just as well not to say anything to his brother about it either. So she said nothing.

Conrad walked her back to the house. His left clubfoot made him adopt a kind of rolling gait. She pretended not to notice, as she could tell he was very sensitive to it. She received the impression he was a badly frustrated young man, overshadowed by his more charming brother.

"Quentin is the big man at Collinwood," he told her with a touch of bitterness. "And when Aunt Erica dies he'll own the major part of the estate. If Aunt Erica ever does die! She's nearly a hundred and the villagers say she is a witch!"

"I had a brief meeting with her," Lara said dryly.

"Then you're aware of what I mean," Conrad Collins said. "Insane and weak as she is, there's a quality of mystery and evil about her."

"The legends are probably mostly due to her extreme age," Lara suggested.

He looked doubtful. "No. I think not. I remember her as she was when I was a child – tall and thin and very formidable. She came marching into Collinwood and gave my father a dressing down. She coolly informed him that unless he deeded her a property she felt should be hers she would wish him dead before the year was out."

Lara gasped. "How could she say a thing like that?"

"You don't know what Aunt Erica was like. She said it seriously. Of course my father paid no attention to her. And perhaps it had nothing to do with her, but he was kicked by a wild stallion just a few days before the year was out and died almost at once. I can tell you it made a strong impression on the servants here. And maybe I've been more respectful of her evil talent since."

They were standing by the entrance to the house now. She said, "Of course it was just a coincidence."

"A coincidence," he agreed. "But what a frightening one. And I could tell you of other cases where Aunt Erica made threats and her spells seemed to work."

Lara listened with growing apprehension. She had a vision of the old crone attacking her in the shadowed closet and later of Catherine's warning that the ancient Erica had placed a curse on her.

She tried to dispel her fears by saying aloud, "This talk of witchcraft is too preposterous. I refuse to believe it."

"Good for you," he said mockingly. "But you've come to a poor place to prove it. Collinwood has a reputation for being the abode of a host of phantoms. This old house is supposed to have seen everything from vampires to werewolves. So better keep an open mind on the subject." His words were spoken humorously, but she suspected there was an undercurrent of something else in them. She went up the silent stairway to her room in a troubled state of mind. She'd been at Collinwood less than twenty-four hours and already she was beginning to worry that coming there had been an error.

Because dinner was the first formal occasion since her arrival at the main house, she carefully selected a favorite rose gown to wear. And she spent more time than usual arranging her hair in neat plaits at the nape of her neck. It was a style that suited her. She had no wish to arouse additional jealousy on Catherine Edmonds' part, but she did want to look her best.

When she entered the living room to join the others for sherry, all eyes turned to her. Quentin left Catherine Edmonds and his brother to come forward with a smile and take her hands in his.

"How beautiful you are tonight," he exclaimed, his pale face bright with pleasure. "This is the ideal moment for me to play the waltz."

She went across the room with him to a table where a small wooden gramophone with a huge metal horn sat. He turned a switch which set a small cylinder spinning and a moment later the lilting music of her father's waltz came from the horn in a reasonably pleasant fashion.

Quentin smiled at her. "Isn't that quite wonderful?"

"It is." Her eyes wandered across the room where Conrad Collins showed a mocking smile and Catherine Edmonds was glaring at her.

They stood there until the record ended and Quentin turned off the machine. Then he escorted her back to the others and handed her a sherry. He talked all the while, showing that he knew a good deal about her father's many musical compositions and truly appreciated them.

She began to forget the doubts she'd had about visiting Collinwood and relax a little. Her eyes wandered to the portrait of a lovely blond young woman with a wistful expression which hung on the paneled wall near her.

She asked Quentin, "Who is that?"

His manner changed at once. He stared at the portrait in a haunted fashion and said, "That is Mary, my late wife. She died very suddenly about two years ago."

"I'm sorry," she said. "It's just that I found her so striking."

Quentin's glance lingered on the portrait. "Yes," he agreed quietly. "She was."

The easy mood seemed to be broken after that. Lara could almost see Catherine's glee at the awkward situation she'd created in mentioning the portrait. As they strolled toward the dining room, Quentin and the dark girl went ahead leaving Conrad and Lara together in the rear.

Conrad gave her a teasing look. "You've learned another subject to avoid," he said. "We never speak of Mary in this house."

"But why?"

"You'll find out," was all the help he gave her.

The gleaming silver, expensive china and candelabra with their tall lighted candles made a charming table but did not break the gloomy mood that had fallen on them all. Catherine was sullen and resentful, Quentin brooding and silent, and Conrad chose to indulge in comments that at the best were acidly humorous. Lara somehow endured them all until the meal was over.

As they were leaving the dining room, Quentin joined her in a penitent mood. Gently taking her arm, he suggested, "Suppose we take a stroll in the garden. It's still very pleasant outside."

"If you like."

They left the others and went out the front door to the garden. They went a little distance along the gravel walk before he said, "I'm sorry I was so difficult at the table. Your mention of Mary's portrait upset me."

"I'm sorry."

"You couldn't have known. One day I'll explain the circumstances to you."

"You needn't if they are so painful."

Quentin gave her a grateful glance. "You're a fine, understanding girl," he said. "I'm glad you're here."

"I've worried that I shouldn't have come."

He paused in their strolling and assured her, "You mustn't have any such thoughts."

She smiled ruefully. "Your Aunt Erica seems to have taken an irrational dislike to me."

"Aunt Erica has had a lifetime of taking irrational dislikes to almost everyone. She's old and senile. You mustn't mind anything she says."

"Catherine hardly fits in the same category," Lara pointed out. "And she resents me."

He raised his eyebrows. "I haven't been aware of it. Are you sure you're not imagining this?"

"She spoke quite plainly to me," Lara said, her eyes meeting his. "It can be no secret to you that she is romantically interested in you. And she is afraid I may threaten any romance between you two."

"But I'm not in love with her," he protested. "I never have been."

"Have you told her that?"

"No. Should it be necessary?"

She smiled faintly. "Young women have a habit of forming love fantasies if they aren't properly warned. I think it would be fair to tell her the truth. Only, now she'll believe I'm responsible for your turning from her."

Quentin's wide set eyes were fixed on hers. "In a sense that's true," he told her solemnly.

Lara blushed. "You can't seriously mean that. We've only just met!"

"But we have written to each other so long I feel I know you well. You have all the beauty and quality of your father's music. You're the sort of girl who could make my life have meaning again."

"Please!" she protested.

"I know this as well as I ever will," Quentin said taking her in his arms. "I love you, Lara." And he gave her a long kiss.

When he released her she looked up at him with anxious eyes. "I like you," she said, "but we mustn't rush into this. Let us give ourselves time to really know each other."

Quentin smiled at her indulgently. "Take as long as you like. You know where I stand now."

"I'm not sure I can bring you happiness," she said, and she stared beyond him up at the old house. Her eyes settled on a window on the third floor. She was positive she saw a curtain flick and the shadow of Aunt Erica's thin witchlike face show in the window momentarily. In a strained tone, she added, "I don't know whether I can live here or not. There's something frightening about the house."

Quentin looked wary. "Frightening? In what way?"

She looked down. "Don't make me try to explain it now. Give me a little time. Maybe later I'll feel differently."

"I should hope so," he said in a subdued, almost cold tone. "I trust Barnabas didn't fill you with a lot of nonsense about this place last night."

This startled her. She raised her eyes to his pale, troubled face. "Not at all. I found your cousin quiet and charming."

A derisive smile played about Quentin's lips. "I'd advise you to avoid him from now on. Otherwise you might have cause to see him in a different light."

Her brow furrowed. "Why do you say that?"

"Barnabas is not what he seems," Quentin told her. "There are some strange rumors about him in the village. If they continue I may have to ask him to leave Collinwood."

She was astonished and a little angry. Barnabas had been much too kind to her for her to have any bad opinion of him. "I can't imagine what the gossip may be, but I'd be willing to say it's not true."

Dusk was quickly settling and she couldn't be sure of the expression on Quentin's pale face. But he listened to her in silence and then said, "I'll talk to you about it at another time."

His words had an absent vagueness to them which caught her attention. She studied him more carefully and saw that he wasn't looking at her at all. A rapt expression had crossed his sensitive features and he was gazing up at the pale full moon gradually standing out against the darkening sky. The moon reflected on the ocean and gave the night an eerie beauty.

It seemed to her his focus on the moon had something abnormal to it. She waited for him to break his staring at the distant silver globe, but he didn't. A tiny feeling of panic started up in her. "What is it? Is there something wrong?"

Only then did he give her an anguished glance. "No, nothing wrong. It's just that I feel one of my headaches gathering." He pressed his hand against his forehead, covering his eyes for a brief moment. Then he removed it to show an expression of utter weariness. "You must excuse me," he mumbled and he turned and hurried off into the growing shadows.

Perplexed and disturbed, she watched him as he vanished behind a hedge, leaving her alone in the garden. He had suddenly seemed in a torment to get away from her.

Darkness was closing down swiftly now and the soft glow of lamplight showed at many of the windows of Collinwood but she continued to stand there, a distance from the huge mansion. From the cliffs she could hear the sound of the ocean as it beat relentlessly against the shore. All the menacing evil of the place seemed to lurk in the shadows around her. She was trembling!

What did these headaches of Quentin's mean? And why had he talked so hostilely about Barnabas and resented the mere mention of the name of his dead wife? Could the attractive, high-strung young man be on the brink of insanity? It was a terrifying possibility.

Surely his ancient aunt was mad. Perhaps a strain of insanity lurked in the Collins family. Yet Conrad seemed to show no signs of it, even if he had a cruel sense of humor. On the other hand his passion for those savage dogs was hardly normal.

She could not accept his insinuations against Barnabas. Had it not been for this cousin, she would have had to turn to strangers for assistance last night. She longed to talk to Barnabas again and realized that he would probably be free to see her now. But where would she find him?

It was as dark as it would be on this moonlit night. She glanced briefly at the pale orb high above her and showing in the ocean. She felt isolated and fearful where she was, but didn't know where to go. She wanted to find Barnabas and didn't think it likely he'd call at the house.

He knew too well how Quentin felt about him.

She heard someone walking towards her and strained to see who it was. A moment later she recognized Catherine Edmonds.

"Where is he?" Catherine demanded imperiously.

"Who?"

"Quentin. I saw him come out here with you," the girl said in a withering tone.

Lara was both annoyed and fearful. There was no telling to what lengths Catherine's passion for Quentin would lead her. She said, "He was only here for a short time. I have no idea where he went."

The dark girl smiled scornfully. "A likely story."

"It's the truth."

Catherine stood there emanating hatred. "You're such a little fool you don't realize if you stay here you're going to die!"

"I don't know what you're talking about!" Lara declared stoutly, not wanting to let the other girl be aware of her fear.

The dark girl's lip curled. "Haven't you seen and heard enough? Do you intend to stay until Aunt Erica's curse begins to work? Then it will be too late!"

"Black magic doesn't frighten me."

"I'd advise you to think about it a second time." Catherine glanced over her shoulder at the old house with its several lighted windows. She pointed to a window high up where Lara was sure she'd seen the emaciated face. "She's up there now, invoking the curse! You can't fight her kind of evil!"

"Yet I do understand yours," she said in a voice much calmer than her state of mind. "You're mad with jealousy! Jealousy of a man who doesn't love you!"

"And let you tell it!" Catherine said angrily. "I'll believe that when I hear it from Quentin."

"I expect you will hear it from him, and soon."

"I have nothing to worry about. The curse will take care of you." With that, Catherine hurried back to the house.

It had been an unnerving experience. But Lara hoped that by standing up to the girl she'd discouraged her from threatening her again. Yet all this talk of a curse being put on her was terrifying. She didn't believe in it and yet it frightened her.

She felt she had no choice but to return to the comparative safety of the old mansion. She'd only gone a few steps along the gravel path when she saw the thing leap out from the bushes and stand straight in her path snarling at her. She gave a sob of fear as she stared into the glittering cat eyes of the phantom wolf of the previous night!

CHAPTER 4

L ast night she'd had the protection of Barnabas and been seated in a carriage. Now she was standing on the gravel path with the snarling monster only a few feet from her, more awesome than ever. She saw the open mouth with the cruel fangs and slavering tongue and knew that it was only a matter of seconds before the wild thing would leap on her.

Hands upraised, she slowly shrank back as the phantom wolf twisted its head and snarled louder and more alarmingly. She watched with horror as it crouched for an attack. And then from the shadows beside her there emerged another figure. It was Barnabas Collins. The man in the caped coat paid no attention to her as he planted himself between her and the gray beast.

She watched in hypnotized fear as Barnabas brought out a pistol and fired at the wild creature. The bullet must have found its mark for the beast gave a howl of pain and went running off into the night. Once sure that the thing had fled, Barnabas turned to her quickly.

"It's all right," he assured her. "Let's get away from here as fast as we can. They'll be coming out to inquire about the shot and I don't want to indulge in explanations."

She nodded mutely, still overwhelmed. He led her around a hedge and out across the lawns to the very edge of the cliff where there was a path. Here in the cover of darkness they halted.

She said, "You came to me again when I needed you."

Barnabas smiled grimly. "It was just chance that I happened to be there. And chance that we met on the wharf."

Lara shook her head. "That giant wolf! Was it the same one we saw last night?"

"It looked a lot like it."

"Could it have been one of Conrad's wild dogs?"

Barnabas appeared skeptical. "I doubt it."

She looked at the black hulk of Collinwood in the distance and gave a small shudder. "Then what kind of evil thing is it?"

"I mean to find that out. In the meantime, I'm satisfied you're safe. How did you happen to be standing out there in the darkness by yourself?"

She looked at him with fear-stricken eyes. "Quentin invited me out there to talk. All at once he complained of feeling ill. He really looked as if something might be wrong with him. He kept staring at the moon. He looked . . . mad. And then he rushed off and left me alone."

"Your first experience of Quentin's illness, if we omit last night."

"The reason he didn't go to the wharf to meet me last night was that he'd written me not to come. Only I'd left before the letter reached my home in Philadelphia."

Barnabas seemed interested. "So your invitation here was actually withdrawn."

"Yes. And I'm sure I would have been better off not to come. Not only is Quentin in a strange state but there is that mad old woman, Aunt Erica, and Catherine, who seems insanely jealous of Quentin."

"You haven't mentioned Conrad?"

"I feel rather sorry for him," Lara said. "He seems nice but very bitter, as if he's always had to play a poor second to Quentin. And there's his bad foot, of course. It's not pleasant to be crippled."

"I agree," Barnabas said. "Do you want to remain here? I can take you down to board the night boat if you wish."

"That would be the easy way," she admitted. "But now that I'm here maybe I should brave this situation out. Otherwise I'm liable to always think of myself as a coward."

"I'd say you were anything but that."

She smiled at him wanly. "Thank you."

Barnabas glanced back towards Collinwood and then said, "I'd like to get a little further away from the house. Suppose we walk along the cliffs to Widows' Hill."

"Whatever you like."

They strolled slowly along in the moonlight. It seemed to her that the handsome man knew a good deal more about what was going on at Collinwood than she had guessed. But apparently he wasn't ready to reveal all he knew as yet.

As they neared the high point of the cliffs she could see the beam of the lighthouse on Collinsport Point. Its shaft of light flashed out across the calm water and swung around in an arc. It would vanish briefly, only to come swinging back again. The steady wash of the waves on the beach below was augmented now and then by the sharp cry of a nightbird. There was a melancholy in the air that seemed to touch on everything.

Barnabas had been walking in silence, his head bent as if in thought. There was a wooden bench set out near the cliff's edge at Widows' Hill and he paused by it. He used his shining black cane to flick a tiny stone over the cliff's edge and then indicated the bench. "You might as well sit down and be comfortable."

"For a few minutes," she said. "I suppose I should go back. They may worry about me." She sat down.

"At Collinwood?" There was a bitter smile on his gaunt face. He stood near her with his back to the ocean.

She gave a tiny shudder. "I can still see that snarling beast. Where do you think it came from?"

"Who knows?"

"It must be wandering on the estate. And not far from Collinwood itself. We weren't all that distance from the main house when it sprang in front of the carriage last night."

"No."

"There seem to be dense woods not far from the house. The creature could be lurking there."

"It could be."

She frowned at his quiet comment and searched his handsome face for some sign of what he was really thinking. She found no clue there. She said, "You believe that Conrad is responsible. That it is one of his dogs. But he insists he has them well trained not to attack without reason."

Barnabas smiled down at her. "You jump to conclusions. I made no accusation against Conrad."

"What are you thinking?"

"Suppose we go back a little further. To before you came to Collinwood. How long have you known Quentin?"

"I first began corresponding with your cousin after my father's death. He'd been writing to my father for several years about his music. And often my father would read me excerpts from his letters. So I came to feel I knew him."

"And no doubt he feels the same way about you?"

She looked down at her folded hands. "I suppose so."

"Has he spoken to you in that vein?" His voice was sharply probing.

Lara glanced up at him. She nodded. "Just a little while ago before he had that spell he told me that he loved me."

Barnabas raised his eyebrows. "Didn't you find that surprising? I mean, after your being here only such a short time?"

She took a deep breath. "I told him it was too soon. That I would need to know him better before making any such important decision."

"I should hope so. What has he told you about his late wife?"

"Mary? He doesn't seem to want to discuss her at all. I happened to notice that painting of her in the living room. When I mentioned it he became angry."

"Interesting. So you don't know how she died?"

There was an ironic undertone to his words that disturbed her. "No. What were the circumstances?"

Barnabas turned to look down where the incoming waves were breaking on the rocks in frothing fury. "Her body was found down there."

"Oh?" She at once became tense. "You mean she was a suicide?"

He glanced at her again, a grave expression on his handsome face. "Hardly. Her throat was ripped open by some kind of animal."

His words caught her with a stunning impact. Bewilderment showed on her lovely face as she stared at him. "Mary was killed by this same wolf?"

"Some wild animal. It happened two years ago. It's a question of whether it was the same one or not."

"No one told me," she said in a low, taut voice.

"My cousin doesn't like the tragedy mentioned," Barnabas said. "The mystery of his wife's death was never solved. She was a wealthy young woman from Boston. I believe her parents were badly upset."

"Of course."

"There was a routine investigation by the local authorities but no solid conclusions were reached," he went on. "At one time there was the suggestion that it wasn't the work of an animal at all. That Quentin's wife had been murdered by a human in a peculiarly brutal way to make it look as if an animal's teeth had ripped her throat. Then the whole thing was abandoned."

The revelation had come as a sickening shock to her. "Were that mad Aunt Erica and Catherine Edmonds living here then?"

"Yes," Barnabas said. "Do you think Erica decided to eliminate Mary, using some of her black magic tricks?"

Lara gave him a reproachful look. "I don't find that amusing. She's already threatened me."

"I'm sorry," Barnabas said and sat down on the bench beside her. "But what I said was not meant to be a joke. Surely you must have heard about werewolves? It's an ancient enough lore. The theory that some individuals can at will turn themselves into wolves or even be changed into wolf form through a curse placed on them."

Her eyes narrowed as she remembered her encounter with Aunt Erica. "Today when I saw her she rambled on about wolves and lycanthropy."

"That bears out what I've been telling you. Erica may not be as senile and unaware as you think. It could be she knows well what is going on here."

Lara stared at the grave, handsome face in disbelief. "You can't be telling me that someone here at Collinwood has the power to change into animal form?"

"The villagers have long claimed that Erica can assume animal form."

"You're not suggesting that snarling,huge wolf and that frail old woman are one?"

"In the Black Arts, anything is possible."

She shook her head. "It's too fantastic!"

"There are many things in this world beyond the comprehension of the average person," Barnabas assured her solemnly. "Don't be too hasty in putting aside any theory."

Lara studied him in silence, a moment. The moonlight highlighted his gaunt face and tinged it with sadness. Then she asked,"Why does Quentin dislike you?"

"Does he?"

"I'd say so. He suggested that I avoid you in the future."

Barnabas was leaning on his cane, which he'd placed before him. "Perhaps Quentin was worried that I'd reveal too much about him."

"Perhaps."

"We have never been close," Barnabas admitted. "But then, my branch of the family has never had a warm welcome here since the first Barnabas Collins left under a shadow."

"What sort of shadow?"

"An ancient scandal. It's not worth mentioning now. But it created a seed of dissension among us that has taken root and grown through the years."

"Quentin said something about you being the subject of village gossip. As if you'd been mixed up in some criminal thing. And he mentioned he might even ask you to leave Collinwood."

Barnabas smiled thinly. "I somehow doubt that he will do that. His own position is far too desperate."

"What is this talk about you?"

He shrugged. "Nothing important. I believe some of the servants have gossiped about me. They don't understand my hours nor my preoccupation with cemeteries. They seem to think any man who wanders about inspecting gravestones in the night is a kind of ogre."

"But this is your own affair."

"I prefer to think so," Barnabas said easily. "My cousin has decided to align himself with the ignorant villagers."

"I let him know I thought he was wrong."

"Thank you."

"I could do no less. You have been so kind to me since my arrival here. And tonight you saved my life. Apparently you wounded that beast. Do you think it might have been fatal?"

He shook his head. "My bullet seemed to strike it in the right front leg. It was holding that foot up as it vanished." He paused. "Concerning the werewolf business, there is a theory that any wound inflicted on the phantom animal will show up in the same place in the human counterpart. You might be well advised to check if any of those at Collinwood have an injured right arm."

She eyed him incredulously. "You're not serious."

"I don't think any angles of this should be ignored," Barnabas told her. "You should know the truth about Quentin and all the rest. It is plain to me he invited you here for one reason only."

"He asked me here to recover from my father's death."

"That was his excuse. But his true reason was that he'd fallen in love with you and wants you to be his wife. It could be that he'll make a worthy husband. But you should be certain of that before committing yourself to him."

Her cheeks burned in her confusion. "I had no such romance in mind when I came."

He frowned. "It is important to remember that Quentin canceled his invitation to you for some reason. Changing his mind was a last minute compromise, largely because you were already here."

"Perhaps Catherine Edmonds persuaded him to do it. She would like to marry him."

"And may know enough about the dark goings-on here to be able to hold it over Quentin's head. Be prepared for her to make other attempts to get rid of you."

"She's already threatened me and asked me to leave."

Barnabas smiled grimly. "You've had a busy and dangerous time since your arrival at Collinwood. Do you think you can go on withstanding the hatreds here?"

"I'm not sure," she said slowly. "Having you to depend on is important. If only I could reach you directly during the days."

"Impossible," he said shortly.

"So I'll have to hoard my problems until the evenings?"

"I'm afraid so." The tall man got up from the bench. "Now I'd better see you safely back to Collinwood."

She rose with him. "I saw that painting in the hallway."

"Good."

"It is very like you."

"I think so," he agreed absently and they began the walk back.

Barnabas accompanied her to within fifty feet or so of the front entrance of Collinwood, then halted to say goodnight. "You must be doubly cautious until we find out some more."

"I understand."

He studied her fondly. "In the short time we've known each other I've come to care for you a great deal."

She smiled up at him. "And I like you, Barnabas."

"Friendship between us may present problems for us both," he warned her. "But I am willing to take the risk if you are."

"I depend on you," she said. "Otherwise I'd leave Collinwood tonight."

"I hope I haven't given you false confidence."

Her eyes searched his face. "One of my chief reasons for remaining here is to know you better."

His answer was to embrace her and press those oddly cold lips to hers in an ardent kiss. She returned the kiss and clung to him for a long moment before they parted. How strange she thought, to have been kissed by two men in one evening. What did she really know about them – and perhaps more important, what did she feel? Suddenly she wanted to be alone, to think.

She left him and hurried across the moonlit lawn to the door of Collinwood. With her hand on the knob she turned to wave him goodnight and was surprised to find that he'd already disappeared. It gave her a strange feeling of depression to realize she wouldn't see him again until after dusk tomorrow.

Opening the door, she let herself into the house. The dimly lighted main hall was silent and empty, the stairway up into the shadows ominously still and waiting. Her heart began to beat a trifle faster as she realized how alone and isolated she was in the old mansion. She looked up at the portrait of the first Barnabas in dark oils and found some solace in its likeness to the charming man she'd just left.

While she was standing there staring at the painting, the oaken door behind her opened slowly. It made her start nervously and wheel around to see Conrad Collins standing there. Quentin's younger brother seemed amused at her shock.

"I didn't intend to scare you."

She drew a sigh of relief. "Don't blame yourself, it's me," she said. "I'm not used to the quiet and isolation of this country place."

"Not to mention my dogs," Conrad said. "You shouldn't be afraid of them. They're not as ferocious as they seem."

"I'm sure of that." She hesitated before she went on to add, "But isn't it natural for strangers to be nervous about them? They are so wolf-like! And Quentin's wife was killed by some sort of wild animal?"

Conrad's pleasant, mustached face shadowed. "Did he tell you he believed one of my dogs killed Mary?"

"No."

"You needn't be afraid to tell me," the young man went on angrily. "It's not the first time he's insinuated it. He tried to make me destroy them all and do away with the kennel."

"It was my own idea," she protested, sorry that she had upset him so. "No one else said anything about it. I'm sure there are plenty of wild animals in the woods here who might attack humans."

Conrad closed the door and limped the few steps over to her, an intense look on his sensitive face. "I've seen panthers within a mile of this house," he said. "And there are wolves left. I've heard them howling on winter nights. And I've seen them standing on a snowy hill, greenish-gray under the moonlight."

"Have you told Quentin about this?"

He looked scornful. "Quentin never listens to me. No one does. I'm the crippled younger brother. The unimportant one. It's always been that way. I tried to tell them when Mary was found with her throat torn open. But all they wanted to do was blame it on my dogs."

She stared at him sympathetically. "You're very fond of those animals."

His eyes met hers passionately. "They are the things closest to me!"

"I think you are wrong in believing that Quentin and the others think little of you," she said. "That is in your own mind. From the moment we met I found you very pleasant."

"But not as pleasant as Barnabas," he suggested with a mocking smile.

"Why do you say that?"

"I didn't intend to spy," Conrad said. "But I was coming this way when I happened on you two having a romantic moment. I didn't want to intrude so I waited in the bushes until you parted."

Lara was blushing furiously. "Barnabas is my good friend!"

"You don't need to explain." He glanced up at the portrait. "No wonder you stopped to study that painting. It could be him, couldn't it?"

"Yes," she nodded, anxious to change the subject. She looked at the portrait again, still deeply embarrassed by Conrad's revelation. "This was the first Barnabas Collins."

"They forced him to leave Collinsport," Conrad said. "But I guess you know all about that."

She turned to him. "No, I don't. I understand he left under a shadow. What was the trouble?"

He seemed amused. "It's hard to realize what a short time you've been here at Collinwood. How little you know about it."

"I'm a good deal in the dark about most of its history."

"So you are." He looked up at the artist's study of that first

Barnabas once more. "He was the one responsible for the vampire legend which has been associated with Collinwood ever since."

Her eyes widened. "Vampire legend?"

He nodded. "It started with an unhappy love affair. This Barnabas was cursed by a girl called Angelique and as the result of a bite of a vampire bat he became a vampire. You know what that means?"

"I've not made a study of the supernatural."

Conrad smiled. "You might find it worthwhile . . . especially if you remain here long. A vampire is one of the living dead. Under the curse, the man or woman is unable to die. They sleep in their coffin during the daylight hours and stalk the darkness in search of human blood. Blood they must have to satisfy their unearthly thirst and keep them content in their twilight lives. The blood is secured through the vampire kiss. And that was the undoing of Barnabas."

She listened to this with increasing horror. "In what way?"

He hesitated a moment, looking grim. "The tender throats of young girls are most attractive to vampires. It is from such throats that much of their blood supply is obtained. Too many village girls were attacked in this manner. And the clues gradually led to Barnabas Collins. He had no satisfactory alibi and so they gave him the choice of prison or leaving. He left. According to the story he went to England and founded a branch of the family."

"But it was all superstitious nonsense!" she protested. "He couldn't have been guilty. There can't be any such things as vampires!"

"The Collins family have always insisted that Barnabas was innocent," he said. "But the villagers have stubbornly stayed with their side of the story. And even now in 1895 they still whisper about seeing vampires on the estate and young girls usually refuse to hire out here as servants."

"But no one would be silly enough to connect the present Barnabas Collins with the legend," she said, at the same time recalling the vague remarks she'd heard from Quentin about the villagers' gossiping.

"On the contrary, there have been some weird accusations made against this Barnabas since he's arrived to stay at the old house."

"Ridiculous!"

Conrad spread his hands. "You know how easily these things get started again? Barnabas prefers to sleep during the day. And at night he often prowls in the cemetery here or the one in the village. Quentin warned him about it but he paid no attention. Now the villagers are talking vampire again."

"Anyone who knows Barnabas would laugh at the idea."

"But none of these people do know him, except to see him strolling about after dark." He paused. "And then there are other things. You must know how cold his hands are."

"Many people have poor circulation!"

"Granted," Conrad said. "But they don't also have nocturnal habits. And there are always hysterical young women in any area who will claim to have been attacked in order to create attention for themselves."

"It all sounds as if the villagers were at fault, not Barnabas."

"That is because you see it from his side," Conrad said with a smile. "If the whispers keep growing Quentin will likely have to ask him to leave. It has happened before."

"I call it most unfair."

"But then you are fond of Barnabas," Conrad said in his mocking way.

They went upstairs together and she was conscious of the difficulty he had in walking. On the whole, she decided she was glad to have this new information. She would no longer be ignorant of the vague references made by Quentin and the others. In a way she would have preferred to have heard the story first from Barnabas, but she could understand his reluctance to discuss the subject.

She said goodnight to Conrad at the first landing and he hobbled off down the dark hall to his own room. She went up the second flight of stairs to the third floor where her room was situated.

The floorboards creaked under her as she moved swiftly down the dark hall. With a small sigh of relief she opened the door of her room and went inside and bolted the door after her. The ceiling lamp had been lighted and there was also a candle, partly burned, flickering in a holder on her bedside table.

The events of the night had left her extremely upset. So many sinister undercurrents were present at Collinwood to thoroughly confuse her. She was sure that small items of fact had again and again been blown up to monstrous legends, that much of the talk of phantoms and murder was exaggerated. Yet there were some things she knew to be true. She had been threatened by the wild wolf-like thing that was lurking on the estate and there was a mystery surrounding the death of Quentin's first wife. And a minor mystery concerning the shadowy illness which he had thought sufficiently serious to warrant canceling his invitation for her to visit Collinwood.

Filled with uncertainty she approached the dresser to remove her jewelry. As she took off an earring and put it down something on the dresser top made her gasp in horror. A tiny black snake with a coil of her blond hair wrapped around its middle had been placed there!

CHAPTER 5

Her startling discovery sickened her. For just a brief second she thought she saw the shining little snake wriggle and then she realized it was a trick of the lamplight. The snake wasn't alive. She drew back from the dresser in revulsion. Of course it had something to do with Aunt Erica and her black magic. It had to be that!

The strands of her hair had been reclaimed from the waste basket. No doubt Catherine Edmonds had helped the senile old woman prepare this disgusting evil charm to terrify her. Catherine, who was so anxious to get her out of the house. Lara stood there directly under the hanging lamp as she debated what she should do.

It was too late to go downstairs and inform Quentin, particularly since he'd complained of illness earlier in the evening. There was only Conrad she could turn to and she'd already said goodnight to him. It became increasingly clear she'd have to let the disgusting thing stay on her dresser for the night and take care of the matter in the morning.

She began preparing for bed and thinking what an evil old woman Erica Collins was. If the witchlike creature had the power, Lara didn't doubt that she would turn herself into the snarling monster of the early evening. Wasn't it Barnabas who'd hinted this might be the case? She'd heard so many fantastic stories her brain was wearied with them.

When she was ready for bed she put out the ceiling lamp but let the candle by her bedside remain flickering. It sheltered her from complete darkness. Staring up into the shadows, she worried about what it all might mean. Conrad's explanation of the vampire legend had explained the mystery surrounding Barnabas. But there were other more terrifying secrets yet to be revealed.

Sleep, when it came, was a thing of troubled dreams. She was pursued by the emaciated Aunt Erica, who held a squirming little blade snake in her bony hand. Reaching her, the old woman cackled madly and abruptly thrust the tiny serpent close to her face. Lara screamed and woke herself up!

The candle at her bedside had meanwhile burned out, so that now she was in total darkness. She lay there filled with stark terror from her nightmare and apprehensive that the ancient madwoman might come stalking her in the small hours. It was true she'd bolted her door, but who knew what mysterious secret passages there might be in a rambling mansion such as Collinwood?

Then she heard the slight movement in the far corner of the room. Paralyzed with fear, she could not call out. And then slowly the figure of Barnabas appeared from the shadows. Her fear gave way to relief and she raised herself a little in the bed.

"Barnabas!" she whispered.

His gaunt face had an expressionless, odd look and his burning eyes fixed on hers. She was hypnotized by them and stared into their depths as he came close to her bedside. He stood there a moment, then reached out and took her bare arms in his icy hands and gently settled her back on the pillow.

His gaze now was of infinite tenderness. She knew no fear and had no thought of protesting. All her will had been subjected to his. Very slowly he bent over her and then his cold lips brushed her neck gently. And that familiar sensation of pain and ecstasy was repeated. She closed her eyes and slept.

It was morning when she wakened, her mind befogged. It took her several minutes to put the macabre events of the previous night in some sort of order. She knew part of it had been a nightmare and part real, but she couldn't separate one from the other. She was certain of one remembered horror, the evil charm left on her dresser. Hurriedly she got up and prepared to go downstairs. Because she avoided the dresser and its mirror, she didn't see that there was a vivid red mark on her throat.

Downstairs the first person she encountered at the breakfast table was Conrad, who heard her story with a look of cool amusement. "I'd suspect Catherine had a hand in that."

"I mean to complain to Quentin."

"You should," he agreed over his coffee. "I think it pretty

fantastic. Locks of your golden hair entwined around a serpent. I wonder what evil that is supposed to work on you?"

"I don't know," she said with annoyance. "But Catherine and that old woman have gone too far this time."

Conrad smiled across the table at her. "Aunt Erica is mild now compared to what she used to be. In her prime she headed a black magic circle in the village. Had a surprising number of the local gentry in it. One of the local parsons denounced her from the pulpit as a filthy creature with black wings. I warn you the Collins family are an infamous lot!"

"Why do you keep her here?"

The young man with the mustache chuckled. "Part family pride and part fear of her, I'd say. Now that she's old and ill she can't live alone. She owns most of the estate, anyway, though she's willing it to Quentin. And since she's supposed to have conjured the death of my father and at least a dozen others, we probably thought she'd invoke a spell on us if we didn't do the proper thing."

"How did you come to engage Catherine Edmonds as her companion?"

"Catherine is the surviving only daughter of one of the gentry I spoke about earlier. Her dear departed father was as firm a believer in Satanism as Aunt Erica. So Catherine was brought up in the tradition, so to speak. Her father left her little else than his mad beliefs, so she was glad to take on the care of Aunt Erica."

"No doubt with the hope of winning Quentin or you as a husband."

"Quentin would be her target," the young man opposite her said. "I don't appear to have his charm where the ladies are concerned." He grimaced. "At least my dogs like me. They don't worry that I'm a cripple."

She paused in buttering her toast to give him a reproachful look. "You make far too much of that."

"Do you think so?" His tone was mocking again.

"Is it your hatred of people that makes you train those poor beasts to be so ferocious?"

Conrad looked pleased. "The thought never struck me. But perhaps you are right. I do dislike most people. At least distrust them. And I've trained my dogs to guard me and my possessions."

"You've probably trained them to be killers."

"Not at all," he said. "Don't let anyone tell you that. And don't you repeat it. I will not have my dogs spoken about badly."

"You're an incredible person. I don't know what to think of you."

He was staring at her with an odd expression on his sensitive face. "Is your throat bothering you this morning?" She returned the stare. "My throat?"

"Yes. No itching or pain?"

"I don't know what you mean," she said, her cheeks crimsoning. "Some insect stung me the other night, but I was sure the mark of it had vanished." She touched her fingers to the spot and was startled to discover a slight swelling there.

Conrad smiled. "I'd watch that," he said. "Bites on the throat can sometimes be dangerous."

Barnabas, she thought. In her bedroom the previous night. He had come over to her and kissed her gently on the throat. But that had been part of her nightmare! It had nothing to do with this tiny swelling.

At that moment Catherine Edmonds appeared in the dining room to take her place at the long table, a distance away from both Conrad and Lara. As the maid came in to serve her, Conrad offered the dark girl a friendly smile.

"We've just been talking about you," he said with roguish recklessness.

Catherine gave him an arrogant glance. "I'm sure it could have been nothing pleasant."

"I was praising you," Conrad went on in his taunting fashion. "I explained to our guest that you were brought up to know all about black magic."

"If I knew that much I'd soon settle with a few people here."

Conrad smiled at Lara. "What are your feelings about Satan's disciples, Miss Balfour?"

"I think we could do with less of them," she said crisply, avoiding the other girl's eyes.

He laughed heartily at this. "You've wit, Miss Balfour. I give you full credit for it." And turning to Catherine again, he asked, "And how is dear Aunt Erica this morning?"

"In a fine temper," Catherine said. "She is engaged in a conjuration and that always makes her content."

"So the old lady's failing health has not spoiled her practicing witchcraft," Conrad said genially. "She must be an inspiration to you."

"I approve of all she does," Catherine said with a malicious look in Lara's direction.

"I would suspect that you direct her activities these days," Conrad went on. "Erica is much too senile to properly instigate such delicate matters on her own. How fortunate she is to have a pretty disciple like yourself."

Lara had listened to enough of this. She rose quickly from the table, her pretty face pale and set, and without a word turned and left the room. The sound of Conrad's mocking laughter echoed after her.

She had an urge to escape from the walls of the grim mansion and so went out into the summer sunshine for a few minutes. Without any particular destination in mind she walked slowly towards the barns. And before she knew it she had come to the kennels.

As usual Conrad's dogs set up a frenzied barking. They sprang against the fence separating her from them and in their snarling aggressiveness indicated they would quickly attack her if they had their freedom. Lara fought her natural fear of the animals and forced herself to move a little closer and inspect them more carefully. She was startled by the resemblance they bore to the wolf-like creature that had roamed the grounds last night and from which she'd been rescued by Barnabas.

Despite Conrad's protests to the contrary, she believed these dogs must be at least part wolf, and capable of killing if they escaped from the kennel. Perhaps they had been responsible for the death of Quentin's wife after all. Lara turned away from the clamoring frenzy of the excited animals and walked back in the direction of the house.

When she reached the gardens she found Quentin standing there, more pale and worn than she had ever seen him before. As she came up to him he told her, "I've been looking for you. I wanted to apologize for last night. I had no choice but to leave you abruptly. I was extremely ill."

She studied him with worried eyes. "You're still very pale."

"I had a very restless night," he said in a low voice.

"What form does your illness take?"

He stared at her. Clearing his throat, he said, "It's rather hard to describe. First I'm stricken with a severe headache. Other symptoms quickly follow. I'm usually prostrated for hours by each attack."

"Have you had medical advice?"

The whiteness of his face made the black side-whiskers stand out. "There seems to be no proper knowledge concerning my condition. It is very discouraging."

"I'm sorry," she said sincerely.

He managed a wan smile. "You mustn't let it trouble you. But now you can understand why I was loath to have you come here."

"Perhaps I should leave," she suggested.

"No." He raised a hand in protest. "I want you to remain."

She felt very sorry for the pleasant young man. It seemed that all the Collins family had some burden to bear. In the face of his illness she hated to bother him about the absurd trick played on her by Catherine Edmonds and his aunt, yet she felt he should know.

She said, "I had an unpleasant surprise when I returned to my room last night"

"Indeed?"

"I think it would be best if I showed it to you," she said. "Do you mind going upstairs for a moment?"

"Not at all."

She led him up to her third-floor bedroom, feeling increasingly uneasy. She had no idea what he would make of the macabre thing which had been left on her dresser. But she hoped he would realize Catherine was to blame and warn her against any repetition of her wicked act. Quentin marched silently at her side.

Entering the room she saw that her bed had been made up. She went straight across to the dresser, but the snake had vanished.

Quentin was standing beside her in front of the dresser. "Well?"

She shook her head in despair. "There was something here I wanted to show you, but someone must have removed it."

Quentin frowned. "What was it?"

"A small black snake."

His eyebrows lifted. "A small black snake?"

She sighed. "I know it sounds crazy, but it's true. There was a small black snake on my dresser last night. It was still there when I got up this morning. A dead snake with strands of my hair twisted around it."

Quentin stared at her. "Are you serious?"

"Quite serious."

"But why?"

"I suppose it was meant to be some evil charm and was put there by either Catherine or your great-aunt. Possibly by both of them."

The young man looked angry. "I can't imagine them doing a dreadful thing like that."

"It was here."

"And you believe the maid took it?"

"She might have."

"We'll soon find out. She must still be on this floor." And he strode out of the room with Lara following him.

They found the maid who had done up her room in Catherine's room a few doors down the hall. Quentin glowered at the frightened girl and demanded, "When you were putting Miss Balfour's room to rights did you find a dead snake on her dresser?"

The maid looked dumbfounded. "No, sir."

Lara couldn't believe what she was hearing. She moved towards the maid, "Didn't you find anything there?"

"No, miss," the girl said nervously. "I just straightened out and dusted. There wasn't anything like a snake there."

Quentin frowned. "I'm sorry to have bothered you," he told the girl. "We must have made a mistake."

When the young man and Lara were out in the hall again, he turned to her and asked, "What do you make of that?"

"I don't know," she confessed unhappily. "It was there.

Catherine must have come back and gotten it when I went down to breakfast. I went down first."

Quentin said, "Do you want me to challenge her about it?"

"She'd only deny it."

"I suppose so." He glanced down to the end of the corridor. "To be truthful it sounds more like something Aunt Erica may have done. She's still strong enough and crafty enough to slip out of her apartment on her own every so often."

"It may have been her," she agreed.

Quentin considered for a moment. "Suppose we go down and pay her a short visit. Catherine was in the living room when we came up here. It's a chance to interview the old woman alone and maybe she'll give herself away."

"Does it matter that much?" Lara asked, not wanting to take advantage of the old woman's senility. She found it all sickening.

His pleasant face showed a grim look. "It could be enough to scare her from doing anything like it again. And don't waste sympathy on her. She has always been a wicked old tyrant."

So it was settled. She followed him down the corridor to the door of the apartment. He knocked and opened it. They went in and Lara was at once amazed by the darkness of the rooms. Apparently Erica insisted on the shutters being kept closed so that only a trickle of light seeped in the windows. They stood there for a moment before there was any hint of the old woman's presence.

Then there came the sound of shuffling footsteps and the thin, crouched figure with the unkempt gray hair came to stand a few feet from them. The old woman swayed slightly as she peered at them through the shadows.

"Is that you, Quentin?" she rasped.

"Yes."

"And is it Catherine with you?"

"No," he said sharply. "It is not Catherine. It is my guest, Miss Balfour. You remember. You intruded in her room the other night!"

The ancient hag cackled. "The blond hussy! I've put a spell on her!"

Standing there in the fetid shadows listening to the madwoman made Lara suddenly feel ill. It seemed to her that much of the evil in Collinwood was centered on this witchlike creature.

Quentin spoke sternly. "I want no more of this nonsense, Aunt Erica. You must keep out of this young woman's room. And we'll have none of your evil charms set out. Do you hear?"

The crone pushed back a strand of gray hair so her emaciated, ugly face showed more. A malicious grin crooked her thin, sunken lips. "Steal forth to churchyards in the night," she rasped. "Themselves to be transformed into wolves. And dig dead bodies up and howl fearfully!"

"I want to hear none of your gibberish," Quentin said angrily. "I've warned you. Unless you behave yourself, you'll be removed to the state asylum!"

The old woman's reaction to this was a gleeful cackle. Quentin took Lara almost roughly by the arm and quickly led her out into the corridor and closed the door after them to muffle the continued mad laughter of the old crone. Thick beads of perspiration stood out at his temples.

"She's the one who played that miserable trick," he said. "She's disgustingly mad and we shouldn't keep her here."

They walked back towards the stairs and on the way met Catherine Edmonds. The dark-haired girl gave them an accusing look. "Have you been up bothering Aunt Erica?"

Quentin frowned. "I had reason to reprimand her."

Catherine smiled sarcastically. "And I can imagine the reason." She looked at Lara. "Can't you find something better to do than bully a senile old woman?"

"I won't try to answer that."

"Because you can't." To Quentin, she added, "Don't expect me to be able to cope with her. I'll not be responsible after you coming up here and upsetting her."

Quentin shrugged. "She should be in a madhouse anyway." And to Lara he said, "Come along."

They left Catherine watching arrogantly after them. And for the first time Lara began to wonder if the forces of witchcraft might be much stronger than she imagined. According to Barnabas, the villagers once believed Erica capable of transforming herself into animal form. Catherine, according to what Conrad had said, was also versed in black magic. Could she not be capable of the same thing? If such things were possible, it opened a whole new avenue of conjectures.

She and Quentin went downstairs together in silence. When they reached the lower hallway, he turned to her and said, "I don't think you need worry about Aunt Erica any more."

"Thank you for what you tried to do."

"You are my guest," Quentin reminded her. "I want you to have a pleasant stay here." As he spoke he raised his right hand and she saw for the first time that it was bandaged.

A feeling of faintness came over her. Last night Barnabas had wounded the snarling phantom wolf in the front right leg and now Quentin was wearing a bandage on his right arm!

Through the blurring confusion she realized that Quentin was staring at her strangely. She raised a hand to her head. "A sudden dizziness," she gasped. "It must be the excitement!"

"Of course," he agreed. "It was an upsetting business up there.

I'm sorry." And he guided her across the hallway to an easy chair by the entrance to the living room.

She sat there for a few seconds and then managed, "I feel much better now."

"Better not try to move around for a little," he warned. "These dizzy spells can return suddenly."

"I'm sorry to be such a bother," she apologized weakly. All the time she was fighting to keep her eyes from that bandaged hand.

"We must try to make things more comfortable for you here."

She took a deep breath and rose from the chair. "I'm fine."

"Perhaps if you took a walk in the air?"

"Yes. That's a good idea." She moved towards the front door.

"I think I'll have your room changed," Quentin went on. "Do you mind? I'd like to get you away from the third floor. It's much too near my aunt's living quarters."

"Whatever you like." And then, since she could no longer keep her eyes from that injured right hand of his, she added, "Did you hurt yourself?"

It was Quentin's turn to appear uneasy. He glanced down at the bandaged hand nervously. "Yes. It happened last night."

"I hope it isn't serious."

"Just a deep cut," he told her. "But I thought I should keep it covered."

"That's wise."

Quentin's face was sickly pale. "I managed to cut myself while opening a wooden crate. I must be more careful in the future."

Lara pretended casualness. "Yes, you should be." Then she went on out.

Perhaps she was being silly, but the coincidence seemed too great to be accidental. Was Quentin truly a werewolf? And was his wound due to the bullet Barnabas had fired at the snarling phantom animal last night? She had an overwhelming desire to see Barnabas and tell him what she had discovered.

She began walking rapidly across the lawn toward the old house. Barnabas had been firm in telling her that he could not see her in the daytime under any circumstances. But this was a very scary turn of events. Surely he would make an exception!

As she neared the vine-covered old house her confidence that he would see her grew. She mounted the stone steps and rapped on the weathered door. It was a few moments before the door swung open and a mildly surprised Benson stood there to greet her.

"Yes, Miss Balfour?" The little man regarded her nervously.

"I'm sorry to bother you, Benson," she said. "But I urgently need to talk to Barnabas."

Benson's round face clouded. "I fear that is impossible."

"But I told you it was urgent," she pleaded.

"I believe you, miss," he said. "But there's nothing I can do about it. I have my strict orders."

"Barnabas will understand when he hears what I have to tell him."

Benson was obviously worried but determined not to give in to her request. "I can't reach Mr. Barnabas at the moment," he said. "But if you'll leave a message with me I'll give it to him as soon as I can."

At once she decided Barnabas must not be in the house. "Tell him I was here and that Quentin has a wound in his right hand. He'll know what I mean."

"Very well, miss," Benson said, looking puzzled.

"You have no idea where I might find him?"

Benson hesitated, then shook his head. "No, miss. It would be better for you to be patient until this evening."

"I can't bear to wait until then," she protested. "A great deal could depend on what he thinks of my information."

"I gather that," the little man said. "But Mr. Barnabas insists on staying with his schedule."

"You will deliver my message as soon as you see him?"

"I will, indeed."

"Thank you, Benson."

She went down the steps again and he closed the door on her. Where could Barnabas have gone? The first place she thought of was the Collins family cemetery. He had mentioned his interest in visiting graveyards and studying tombstones. What more likely place to find him?

Instead of returning to Collinwood she took the path down over the hill to the cemetery on the fringe of the woods. She had never visited it before but this was as good a time as any. Her spirits lifted a little; surely she'd find Barnabas there.

The cemetery was a fairly large one, much larger than it had seemed from a distance. An ornate iron fence surrounded it. Because it was located on a hillside the gravestones and tombs were at different levels. She hesitantly made her way through the open gate and found herself among the neat grassy mounds of the dead. An eerie quiet hung over the burial ground. She picked her way between the forest of granite stones and then paused to gaze around her and see if she could see any sign of Barnabas. But he was nowhere in sight.

She was standing near one of the large tombs which had an iron entrance door and steps leading down to it. Suddenly a creaking of rusty hinges caught her horrified attention and she fixed her eyes on the ancient metal door of the tomb. A chill of terror rushed through her. Very gradually, the iron door was being pushed open.

CHAPTER 6

Terrified as she was, Lara could not take her eyes from that slowly opening door. It seemed that one of the dead had tired of the rotting coffin and cobwebbed darkness and was lifting a bony hand to grope out into the sunlight again. She stood there motionless and holding her breath, waiting for a glimpse of who-knew-what mildewed horror of ragged shroud and grinning skull! Then the door swung back all the way and she fainted.

She opened her eyes to look up into the earnest face of a young man in a dark plaid suit and wearing a cap of the same material.

"You're not a ghost?" she asked plaintively.

"I should hope not," he said in a pleasant voice. "I'm afraid I gave you a fright."

She stared up at him. "Was it you in the tomb?"

He smiled embarrassedly. "Yes. Stupid of me. I found the door ajar and went in to inspect the place. Never been in a tomb before. But while I was in there the door swung closed. Gave me a bit of a start."

Lara raised herself up on an elbow. "And you gave me a worse one. I almost died of fright."

"I know," the young man said contritely. "I can't forgive myself."

"And I'm not liable to forgive you either," she said ruefully. She struggled to her feet and he quickly helped her.

"I saw you as you fell," the young man said. "I came to you as quickly as possible."

Her smile was wan. "The harm had been done then."

"Seeing you gave me a shock, too," he said. "I didn't think there would be anyone in this place but me."

"People often come here," she said. "I came looking for someone. A man wearing a caped coat. Did you by any chance see him?"

The young man shook his head. "No. I've been here for more than an hour and I've seen no one – at least, not until you turned up."

She sighed. "Then I guess he didn't come here."

The young man glanced around. "Interesting cemetery," he said. "The Collins family burial ground. Some of the stones are very old."

Lara was studying him. He seemed a pleasant young man. His features were good but undistinguished. He certainly wasn't one of the locals; he had the stamp of the city on him. A certain air of assurance.

She said, "Are you a friend of any of the Collins family?"

"I'm afraid not," he confessed.

"You understand this is a private cemetery?"

"Yes," he said with a smile. "I'm a trespasser."

"The Collins family don't generally take a light view of trespassers," she warned him.

"Surely they wouldn't object to my coming here," he said in a good-natured tone. He indicated the various graves with a wave of his hand. "None of these people have complained."

She smiled ruefully. "It might be wise to ask permission of Mr. Quentin Collins or his brother, Conrad, before you wander onto their property again."

"Thanks," he said. "I'll remember that. My name is Michael Green and I've come to stay in Collinsport for a few months for my health."

"I'm sure you've picked a good place," she said. "My name is Lara Balfour. I'm a guest of the Collins family."

"Glad to know you, Miss Balfour," the young man said, shaking hands with her. "I'm not enjoying the grandeur of Collinwood, but I do have a nice room in the local hotel."

"I'm from Philadelphia," she said. "And I find it much cooler here in Maine. Where do you come from?"

"Boston," he said. "It gets warm in summer also. About this man in a caped coat you were looking for. Would he be Quentin Collins?"

She laughed. "No. It's his cousin, Barnabas Collins. He lives in the old house up on the hill."

The young man seemed interested. "Of course, I've heard about him. I was told he never leaves that house in the daytime. He wanders around at night. Comes to the Blue Whale Tavern in the village occasionally, and is quite a favorite with the ladies."

Lara was amused. "Barnabas is handsome."

The young man's brown eyes twinkled. "And a favorite with the local girls, if all the gossip is true. They do claim he has a fondness for graveyards, so you are looking in the right place for him. But you should wait until the evening."

"I hoped he might be here now."

"Well, at least it gave us a chance to meet," Michael Green said in his friendly way. "I enjoy talking to someone from the city. Conversation with the villagers is pretty limited. These Maine people have a distrust of strangers. Even from as close a place as Boston."

"I know what you mean."

"This isolated village is like another world," he said. "And I guess the Collins family rule a good part of it."

"They own the fishing factory and a lot of local property."

"And like all ruling families, they've developed some strange quirks over the years."

She was at once on the alert. It struck her that in a nice way this pleasant stranger had been gradually getting a great deal of information from her. Was this accidental or deliberate? And what could his interest be in the Collins family?

She spoke guardedly. "I'm not sure I understand you."

He raised his eyebrows. "Don't tell me you're a guest here and you haven't learned the reputation of this place?"

"What exactly do you mean by that?"

"Collinwood is a place of legends. It's supposed to be haunted. All kinds of ghosts and phantoms are said to have been seen here."

"I pay little attention to such stories."

"And there's an old woman living in the main house the villagers claim to be at least a century old. And they say she's a witch. All her life she has dabbled in black magic. That's why she's outlived all her contemporaries."

Lara frowned. "They mean Quentin's great-aunt. She is old and a little mad , but I doubt that she's a witch."

"I'm only repeating gossip," he told her. "There's talk about your friend Barnabas being a throwback to an ancestor who was a vampire. The villagers are wondering if he's also one of the living dead."

"You should be too intelligent to believe such stories," she said with scorn.

Michael smiled. "I didn't say I believed them. I'm just repeating what I've heard."

"Idle talk of idle tongues."

"Undoubtedly," he agreed. "But listening to the stories passes the time. And I became so interested I decided to stray out here. The best story of all is about the werewolf that's supposed to haunt the place."

Lara tried to hide her uneasiness. "I find the stories all much alike."

The young man's eyes had suddenly grown hard. And he was staring straight at her. "But there's some substance to this one. Your host, Quentin Collins, had a wife die under mysterious circumstances. She was found on a beach with her throat ripped open by some savage beast. Did you know that?"

"Yes," she said faintly.

"No one has ever been able to explain what happened," Michael went on. "Nor was the animal ever found who tore open that lovely throat!"

"They say there are wolves in the area."

His smile was grim. "The villagers say there is a werewolf. And because of what happened I find the possibility fascinating."

Lara stared at him and it occurred to her that all their previous conversation had been leading up to this. "What does it mean to you?"

He continued to smile. "I'm a student of unsolved murders. It is my hobby. And never before have I happened on a case where the murderer is reported to have been a werewolf. It's a challenge to me."

"I see."

"In a purely amateur way," he hastened to add. "I am here for my health. But I enjoy taking stock of local happenings."

"You've made that plain."

He went a few steps from her and studied a weathered gray headstone. "Josiah Collins," he read from it. "The rest is too worn to make out clearly, but I'd say that was one of the older graves."

She said, "I think I'll go back to Collinwood." Somehow he made her vaguely uneasy.

"I'll walk along with you," he said jauntily. "I hope we may become friends and that I'll see you again. We have a mutual interest, the Collins family."

"I'm not sure that I'll be staying here much longer," she said, as they walked through the cemetery gate to the field.

He gave her an inquiring glance. "No? I wondered if you might have come for a long while. If you were going to be the new Mrs. Quentin Collins."

Before she could answer, from up on the hill there came a sudden sharp barking. Instinctively Lara glanced in the direction from which the sound had come and saw Conrad Collins standing there with a gun under his arm. He'd had a dog at his side, but now the great animal was bounding down over the hill toward them, barking furiously.

She gave the young man at her side a frightened glance. "Be careful!"

The words had barely escaped from her lips when the wild gray dog came springing at them, his cruel white fangs revealed in his snarling frenzy. Leaping on Michael, the dog sent him stumbling backward. The young man cried out in fear and fought to protect himself.

Lara screamed and turned toward Conrad for help. "Please! Hurry!"

Quentin's clubfooted brother was making his way toward them at a fairly rapid rate, an ugly look on his mustached face. He went over where the snarling gray dog had Michael Green pinned to the ground and grasping the dog by the collar, pulled him away.

"Down, Caesar!" he ordered the maddened animal. To Lara's surprise the big dog whimpered and obeyed him. With the dog quieted, Conrad went over and helped a rumpled Michael Green to his feet. "You're all right," he snapped.

The young man retrieved his cap from the ground and straightened his tie. His face was grim. "No thanks to Caesar."

Conrad's smile was cruel. "My dogs are taught to attack strangers. What are you doing here?"

"Looking around," Michael Green said defensively.

"Next time do your looking around somewhere else."

Lara spoke up. "This is Michael Green. He's visiting Collinsport for his health."

"It won't improve if he comes spying around here," Conrad said sharply. "Is he a friend of yours?"

She flushed. "We've just met."

Conrad turned to the stranger again. "My name is Conrad Collins and I'm speaking for myself and my brother when I tell you we don't encourage trespassers. I'll give you exactly one minute to be on your way. If you don't like that, I'll put Caesar on you again."

Michael Green stared at him for a moment. "With that choice I'll leave at once. Good day, Miss Balfour. I'm sure we'll meet again." And he tipped his cap to her and turned and began walking smartly up the hill.

Conrad Collins was scowling after him. "Fresh city type," he said. "We know how to handle them."

"I don't understand why you were so rude to him."

He gave her a bitter look. "If we catered to every trespasser that came here we'd have the grounds crawling with people. It's the only way to have privacy. Let them know they're not wanted."

"You certainly did that." She watched the slim figure of Michael Green vanish over the top of the hill.

"Where did you meet him?"

She gave Conrad a reproachful glance. She'd thought him the most human one in the big mansion. Now she wasn't so sure. "We met in the cemetery."

"What was he doing there?"

"I don't know. Reading the gravestones. Some people enjoy that."

"I didn't like him."

"How could you tell anything about him? You chased him away."

There was a mocking gleam in Conrad Collins' eyes as he fitted his rifle under his arm. He leaned over and patted the head of the chastened gray dog. "Come on, Caesar," he said. And he and the dog went on their way.

Lara watched them head towards the woods for a long minute and then with a sigh she went on in the direction of Collinwood. Nothing had worked out as she'd hoped. She hadn't been able to locate Barnabas and so she must patiently wait to see him after dusk. And then this mysterious young man had been sent packing by Conrad before she'd been able to find out much about him.

One thing was sure. He knew a lot about Collinwood and the ghostly legends that had been woven around the old estate, and he had shown a special interest in the tragic death of Quentin's wife. It was plain the young man felt she had been murdered. Lara now had a kind of wild theory of her own. If Quentin really was under the curse of being a werewolf, he had probably murdered the lovely Mary. The question was, would he have done it deliberately or had it been an act he couldn't control in his demonic form? That was one of the questions she must put to Barnabas.

She neared the big house with its tall chimneys stretching to the sky like thin arms and was astonished at the change in her thinking since she'd arrived at Collinwood. She'd never pretended to have any interest in the supernatural. And now she was calmly accepting the fact that Quentin Collins could be a werewolf. Not calmly accepting it, perhaps, but at least willing to believe it was possible.

When she went into the house Catherine came down the stairs. "Your room has been changed."

"Thank you."

"Don't thank me," the dark girl said. "I wouldn't have done it for you. It was Quentin's idea. He has had the maids transfer all your things. You'll be on the second floor. The third door to the right. It's the room next to Quentin's," Catherine went on with a nasty smile.

"Mary slept there until her death." She swept on into the living room, leaving Lara no happier about the choice of her new room.

Lara mounted the stairs and went along the wider first floor corridor to the open door of the room. It was larger than the one she'd previously occupied. And the furniture was French Provincial with a rich crimson rug on the floor and heavy crimson drapes at the windows.

She saw a door that apparently connected her room with Quentin's; it was carefully bolted on her side. This was a relief. And really, the room was much more pleasant than the one on the floor above and had the advantage of not being so near Erica's quarters. Whether Mary had slept in this room or not really made very little difference. Catherine had been trying to make her miserable.

Her window overlooked the gardens and she could also see some of the barns. It was quiet and in the afternoon she took a short nap. Her sleep had been so broken the previous night that she needed this extra rest. She put on a favorite orange dress for dinner and went downstairs to join the others at six.

As she reached the foot of the stairs she heard her father's waltz being played on the gramophone in the living room. She went in and found Quentin standing by the machine alone. He seemed lost in listening to the music and took no notice of her entering for at least a full moment. Then he waved for her to come and stand by him to hear the record through.

When it ended he snapped off the machine and said, "What a lovely tune. Did I ever tell you that Mary heard it just before her death and was entranced by it?"

"No, I don't believe so," she said. She was astonished that he should so casually mention his late wife's name. Until now he had avoided any discussion of her.

"You look very lovely tonight," he said, studying her with appreciative eyes.

She smiled demurely. "I enjoy dressing for dinner."

"We live a simple life here," he told her. "But I do insist on a few of the niceties. Dressing for dinner is one of them. We don't want to sink back to being completely primitive."

"I hardly think that likely in this lovely house."

Quentin looked pleased. He touched his bandaged hand to a side-whisker and she was reminded of all that again. She found herself longing for the hours to pass when she would see Barnabas. Only a little wait now.

Quentin said, "I trust you find your new room an improvement?"

"Yes. I like it."

"I have the room next to it. If you have any reason to call on me for help please remember that. I want you exposed to no more unpleasant incidents."

"I'm sure there won't be any."

He frowned. "Watch Catherine. She is a strange, vindictive girl brought up in a weird fashion. I see now that I made a serious error in introducing her to this household. But I needed someone to care for my aunt and she seemed ideal for the purpose."

"I'm sure she is."

"She seems to have become oddly possessive of me," Quentin worried. "I must ask you to overlook any strangeness on her part."

"I will," she promised.

The young man hesitated and stared at her for a long silent moment. Then, too casually, he said, "There is one other little matter."

"Yes?" Had he noticed her unusual interest in his bandaged hand? Was there to be a crisis concerning that even before she could speak to Barnabas?

"I understand you met a stranger on the grounds this morning."

"I did."

"My brother told me about it. Said the fellow was a rather suspicious character."

"I'd hardly call him that," she said with a wan smile.

"You met him in the cemetery?" Quentin's eyes were boring into her.

"Yes."

"What were you doing there?"

He had caught her by surprise. She could hardly tell him she was looking for Barnabas to discuss that bandaged hand with him. Lamely, she said, "I'd heard about it and decided I wanted to see it."

Quentin's smile was cold. "An odd place for one so young and lovely as yourself to frequent. By the way, you won't find my wife's grave there. Mary's parents insisted that they have her interred in their family plot in Boston. They were so grieved by her tragic death I couldn't find it in my heart to refuse them."

"That was considerate of you."

"I'm telling you this because you might have been looking for her grave and would think it strange not to discover it."

"I wasn't looking for any grave in particular."

"No," he said with another of those cold smiles. "You merely were in a cemetery mood."

"Something like that."

"And so was this young man," Quentin said with irony, "in a cemetery mood."

"I believe he had heard a lot about Collinwood in the village and wanted to see it for himself."

"Probably," Quentin said. "His name is Michael Green, I believe."

"Yes."

"Did he ask you a lot of questions?"

"Not really," she said cautiously. "He didn't have too much time. Conrad put his dog on him and then sent him on his way."

Quentin smiled coldly again. "That may seem harsh to you but I promise you such action is justified on our part. We have been bothered too much by tramps."

"Michael Green is not a tramp."

"No. I'm sure he isn't," Quentin observed dryly. "What I would like to know is exactly who and what he is and why he was sneaking around here."

"I'd say it was nothing more than idle curiosity," Lara said. "He is in Collinsport for his health."

"Interesting."

The others joined them and they all went in to dinner. Lara found herself with little appetite. The minutes seemed to be ticking by in her head. She paid scant attention to the talk of the others, making answers only when she was forced to. And as soon as the meal ended she hurried from the dining room and went outside.

It would be at least a half-hour until dusk. But she had no desire to return to the house until she had met Barnabas. So she walked toward the cliffs and took the path that led to Widows' Hill. The sky was clouding over; it looked as if it might rain at any time. She hoped to be able to contact Barnabas before the storm broke. Hesitating part way along the path, she looked back toward Collinwood. For a moment she'd had a weird sensation of being followed. But there was no sign of anyone coming after her.

She studied the stark lines of the grim old mansion, wondering once again what evil might be going on within its walls. On the third floor there was the senile old Erica, still intent on her sorcery, and Catherine, sullen and willing to help her. Conrad was a problem of a different kind. Sensitive because of his crippled foot and frustrated at always playing second to Quentin, he had turned into an eccentric. He loved his dogs and hated almost all else.

But it was Quentin himself who offered the strangest enigma. She had seen him in a half-dozen moods, and she still felt she knew little about him. On the basis of that bandaged hand she had decided he could be under the curse of the werewolf and the monster that Barnabas had wounded the previous night. But she could be grievously wrong.

A drop of rain hit her forehead and she saw that the skies were blacker and more threatening than ever. She decided that she had better make straight for the old house and meet Barnabas there. He would surely be looking for her. And by the time she reached there it would be dusk.

It was a race between her and the rain and increasing darkness. Fortunately the drops of rain were still scattered but they could become a downpour any moment and she had nothing to protect her from a drenching.

Breathless, she reached the steps of the old house and knocked frantically on the door. It was opened almost immediately by Barnabas. His handsome face showed concern as he saw her.

"You look frightened to death," he said, standing back for her to enter the shadowed hallway.

She nodded. "I've had a bad day."

"Benson told me you were here," he said. "I'm sorry I wasn't able to see you. He gave me your message. Come in by the fire and tell me all about it."

He led her into the comfortable living room of the old house and she sat in a chair before the blazing-log fire and went over it all in detail. Barnabas leaned against the fireplace listening with a frown on his handsome face.

When she had finished, he said, "So you really believe that Quentin may be a werewolf?"

"Yes. What do you think?"

He surprised her by saying, "I've suspected it for some time. Since Mary's death. I believe he murdered her."

"Oh, no!" she gasped.

"It's the logical conclusion if you accept what he is," Barnabas said calmly. "Quentin has an idea I know about him and that is why he doesn't like having me around."

"He's suspicious of everyone."

"I'm sure of that," Barnabas said.

"How can we find out about him for sure?"

"That won't be easy," Barnabas said grimly. "I'll have to give it some thought. And I also want to make sure you're in no danger."

"Why should he want to harm me?"

Barnabas gave her a steady look. "It is possible, even likely, that these spells he has are the times when he takes on the form of a werewolf. And it is also likely that he has no recollection of his actions when he is in this transformation. In other words, the beast could attack and kill and Quentin wouldn't remember it. Nor would he have deliberately conceived the attacks. Once the beast is in possession, the personality of Quentin has no control over it."

She listened with growing fear. "He becomes a mad animal."

"That is what we must assume we are dealing with," Barnabas said gravely. "A mad animal."

CHAPTER 7

In the moment that followed, a vivid blue flash of lightning showed in through the windows of the elaborately paneled living room. The lightning blazed blue across Barnabas' face, highlighting it eerily. When the crack of thunder died, rain drummed heavily against the window panes. Lara realized she was trembling.

Barnabas wore a sober expression. "I still wonder if you shouldn't leave here at once."

She shook her head, not ready to tell him that her feelings for him was one of the main reasons for wishing to remain at Collinwood. So she compromised by saying, "I don't want to leave until I know the whole truth. I'd never be satisfied if I did."

Barnabas lifted an eyebrow. "I expect the truth may not be pleasant."

"I can't help that," she said as another blue flash of lightning and a roll of thunder came.

He frowned. "This stranger you spoke of, this Michael Green, interests me."

"I'd say he knows a lot about Collinwood."

"But why should a stranger have such an interest in the estate and know so much about its people? Doesn't that strike you as odd?"

"I don't know," she said hesitantly. "This is the most imposing house in the area. And as one of the wealthier families you are bound to be talked about."

"But this fellow knows many more facts than the average visitor, it seems," Barnabas said sharply. "How did he impress you?"

It was a difficult question. She wanted to be honest with Barnabas and she didn't want to hurt his feelings. Trying to sort out the proper words, she told him, "I think this Michael Green is smart. And it is probably the legend of Collinwood that fascinates him."

"I wonder," he said thoughtfully.

"He talked a lot about Quentin and the death of his wife. The odd manner of it."

"All that tends to make me suspicious," Barnabas said. "I thought Mary's murder had all but been forgotten."

"Not with the villagers."

"I suppose not."

"They have long memories in such things," she pointed out. "And no doubt the stranger received most of his information in the village. He has a room there."

"And then he comes spying out here."

The lightning flashed again, briefly augmenting the subdued candlelight of the room for seconds. When it and the thunder following it had passed, Barnabas began to pace up and down before her, his head slightly bowed in thought.

She felt she should put in a good word for the young man, who had struck her as being pleasant. "I'd hardly dub him the type to come spying. I do think he wanted to see the house and the cemetery."

Barnabas flashed her a cynical glance. "I find a cemetery an odd preoccupation for a young visitor from the city."

Lara's smile was both rueful and teasing. "But you are interested in cemeteries. Why should you find this strange in someone else?"

He halted before her again. "It's different with me."

"Why?"

Some emotion Lara couldn't interpret flickered across his gaunt face. After the briefest of pauses, he said, "I am one of the family."

"I hardly think that should make all that difference."

"You seem to favor this Michael Green," Barnabas said accusingly.

"I just don't see anything sinister behind his actions."

"That remains to be proven."

There was a hint of disappointment on Lara's pretty face as she sat back in the tall chair. "I expected you to be fairer than the others, but you seem to be showing much the same attitude as Quentin and Conrad."

Barnabas stood before the fireplace with a thin smile on his gaunt, strong face. "I'm sorry. I usually try to be fair."

"I know. I have come to depend on you," she said. "That is why what you said just now came as a shock."

He came over to her and took her hand in his. The chill of his cold touch brought a recollection of the rumors she had heard about him. The lightning came again, this time not so bright, and the thunder that followed seemed distant.

Barnabas studied her fondly. "I would not want to ever cause you to lose faith in me."

"That's not likely."

He still held her hand. "My position in all this is strange. Though I am a visitor, I am also one of the family. But neither Quentin nor his brother really want me here."

Her eyes met his solemnly. In a low voice, she suggested, "I suppose it is because of the whisperings."

"The whisperings?" he asked rather sharply.

She nodded. "You must be aware of them. The villagers think you strange. They link you with your ancestor, the first Barnabas Collins."

Barnabas frowned. "You've never spoken openly to me of this before."

"I think I have hinted about it." The pressure of his cold hand on hers was a constant reminder of her fears. "We both accept that Collinwood is a strange place. Perhaps even a cursed place. And that Quentin may be a werewolf and Erica a witch. What about you? Have you escaped or are you under some dark shadow?"

The hypnotic, burning eyes of the man standing by her in the candlelit room stared deeply info hers. "I'll have to answer that question with one of my own," he said.

Her voice was low as she was caught up in the spell of his great charm. "Please go on."

"Do you think I would ever harm you?"

She did not hesitate. "No."

"Are you willing to go on believing in me without asking questions of any kind about my personal life?"

"If that's what you want."

"It's what I must have from you," Barnabas told her very seriously. "Otherwise I can't help you."

"Have it your way," she said quietly. "I'm sure there is some mystery about you I do not understand, and that you have not tried to explain. But until the other questions are cleared up that can rest."

Barnabas smiled. "Now you are being a sensible girl," he said. And he bent down and touched his cold lips to her forehead in a tender, brief kiss. Then he straightened and moved back before the fireplace once more.

"What about Quentin?" she asked.

"I'm going to try to find out some things about him," Barnabas promised. "There are several avenues I'd like to explore, people who know about him I'd like to talk to. I have only the nights to make such inquiries so it may take a little time."

Her eyes showed fear. "You seem fairly certain he did murder Mary."

"When under the werewolf curse," Barnabas said carefully. "In that transformation he might have done it without intention. On the other hand he may be guided by evil continually. It is one of the things we have to discover."

"He arranged to have my room changed next to his. Because of Erica being on the third floor."

"The question is, should you fear him more than her?"

"He has been very upset by the way Erica and Catherine have acted toward me," she pointed out. "He certainly appears to be my friend."

"As long as you keep in mind it may only be appearance."

Lara gave a deep sigh. "I have become so very confused. I've always liked Conrad and sympathized with him. But I find he's very bitter."

"Because of his being crippled," Barnabas suggested.

"And there is a jealousy of Quentin. It's pretty obvious. He seems to get his only happiness from those brutes of dogs."

"Cousin Conrad presents an interesting study," Barnabas agreed. "But I see him as a minor character in all this."

"I suppose so," she said, rising. "It's late. I should return to the house. Quentin resents my coming here."

Placing an arm around her, Barnabas suggested, "Perhaps he's afraid of losing you to me."

She was thrilled by his closeness and her attractive face brightened. "I have never denied that I like you."

His arm tightened about her. "And my feelings towards you are special," he said.

Lara stared up at his gaunt, somewhat sallow face with the lock of black hair streaking romantically across his high forehead. She said, "Most nights I even dream about you. I imagine you are in my room. And that you come to my bedside, bend down and kiss me on the throat."

His burning eyes never moved from her. "A strange dream."

"I've never had one like it before," she said rather shyly. "The kiss is so real I can almost feel it. It's even vivid to me now. Like a sweet pain."

"You are under too much tension here," he cautioned her. "You must try and manage to sleep more soundly without dreams."

He paused with a weary smile of his own. "Even though I've been lucky enough to be in them."

She stared up at him dreamily. "Barnabas, how old are you?"

He hesitated. "Why do you ask?"

"I don't know. I suppose it's when I think of us. I worry that you may be too old to be really interested in me."

He smiled. "Never worry about that. As to the way I feel about my age, it varies with my mood. There are moments when I feel like a youth and others when at least the weight of one or two centuries seems to burden my shoulders."

They moved on out of the softly-lighted dining room into the murky shadows of the hall, his arm comfortingly around her. For just a little while the tensions and threats of Collinwood slipped from her and she was a young woman, happy and perhaps in love. She enjoyed the brief interlude of bliss to the fullest, knowing it could not last.

In fact, it dissipated as Barnabas halted a short distance from the front entrance of Collingwood. The rain had stopped but the sky was still overcast and it seemed ready to storm again. She glanced at the few squares of amber showing the lighted windows of Collinwood and gave a tiny shiver.

"I'm really frightened about leaving you and going in there," she told him.

He looked down at her solemnly. "But remaining was your decision. I've offered to see you safely on the riverboat many times."

She smiled wanly. "And I've always refused," she admitted. "My curiosity overrules my good sense. What a strange murky turmoil I was thrown into by Quentin's interest in my father's music. I'm almost sorry that waltz became so popular."

"But then we would never have met."

"There is that."

"You don't sound altogether happy," he chided her.

She frowned. "I worry about you."

"Don't," he said. "Whatever happens, I'll manage."

"I want to believe that!"

"Do," he insisted. And he kissed her a final goodbye. Just as she was about to leave him to go to the great mansion, he added, "One other thing, Lara. Don't be too quick to take that Michael Green into your confidence. I'd like to know some more about him."

"I'll remember," she promised.

She hurried along the wet gravel to the door and quickly let herself inside. Once in the hallway she peered out the narrow window next to the door to see if Barnabas had gone. He had. She let the curtain fall back in place and sighed. At the same instant there was a footstep behind her. She turned in mild fright to see Quentin standing there, white-faced and angry.

"Well," he said coldly, "were you out with Barnabas or that

Michael Green?"

"What do you mean?" she asked, pretending innocence.

"Don't lie!" Quentin said scornfully. "You weren't out on this stormy night alone."

"I did go out alone," she maintained stoutly.

"And who did you meet?"

Lara faced up to his rage. "I don't think I have to tell you that," she retorted. "When I accepted your invitation to come here as your guest I fully expected to be treated as one. To have reasonable freedom."

Quentin was clenching and unclenching his fists. "And when I invited you I hardly thought I would find you conspiring against me!"

"But I haven't been!"

"That Green fellow is up to no good," Quentin went on angrily. "What lies has he told you about me?"

"None!"

"I'd like to believe that!" Quentin's harsh, rasping voice was oddly unlike his own, and his eyes held a mad intensity that terrified her. It was a lunatic's blurred glare which he directed at her and yet he hardly seemed to be seeing her at all.

"Please!" Lara said fearfully and attempted to get by him.

He blocked her way. Then she saw the twitching at the corners of his mouth, barely noticeable at first but soon becoming more marked. He raised his hands and in horror she noted that his fingers were clenched in like an animal's paws. His breathing had become frenzied and he swayed slightly.

Then with a sharp cry of pain he clutched at his arms with his hands. As they criss-crossed his chest, he bent as though in agony. Lara drew back against the door and watched in frozen terror. He bent double and then groaning turned and staggered weakly down the dark hall toward his study door. Entering he slammed the door shut after him.

Lara relaxed and gave a long sigh. It had been an incredible experience. Now that her immediate fear had vanished she felt a sincere sympathy for the tormented Quentin. Surely the stories he'd told her of his being ill were well-founded. It was too bad he'd worked himself into an attack. Yet she couldn't blame herself. She felt she had been in the right.

She hurried upstairs to her new room on the second floor, her heart pounding with excitement as she made her way along the shadowed hall. And she remembered that Quentin occupied the room adjoining. With him in his strange, upset state it wasn't a comforting thought.

She touched her hand to the doorknob of her room and all at once was filled with the eerie conviction that there was someone waiting for her on the other side of that door. She stood there for a long moment. Her first impulse was to leave quickly and hurry downstairs. But Quentin was down there! She did not want to risk encountering him again.

Calling on all her courage, she made herself stand there quietly. And as she did so an unexpected sound came from the living room below. It was the haunting waltz of her father's which was such a favorite of Quentin's. Either he or someone else was playing the recording on the gramophone down there. The music came to her in a weird, ghostly manner.

She made a decision. Turning the knob, she opened the door and entered the bedroom in which Quentin's wife Mary had slept until she was murdered. At first the room seemed empty. A lamp burned at either end of the dresser casting a warm glow over everything. She stood there staring about her and after a moment's hesitation closed the door leading to the hallway.

As soon as she did this one of the other doors in the room slowly began to open. It was the door to the larger closet. Lara was hypnotized by the gradually opening door until the figure of a woman was revealed standing there in the shadows. Thoughts of a phantom pressed in on her. Could she be seeing the ghost of Quentin's murdered wife? And then the figure emerged from the closet and she saw that it was Catherine.

Finding her voice, she demanded, "What are you doing here?" It occurred to her that Catherine was up to some of the black magic tricks devised by the mad Erica . . . probably placing some gruesome relic there for her to find.

Catherine was wearing a pale green dressing gown and her long black hair was tumbling about her shoulders. The dark girl looked frightened. Coming across the room to Lara, she said, "I want to talk to you."

"It wasn't necessary for you to hide in here to do that."

"I wanted to speak to you in private," Catherine said. "I didn't want anyone in the house to see me here. I wasn't sure it was you coming into the room so I dodged into the closet until I was certain."

There was a ring of truth in the girl's words that made Lara change tactics. "What is it you have to say to me?" Catherine looked at her earnestly.

"Are you in love with Quentin?"

She frowned. "Why do you ask?"

"I need to know."

"Do you think I'd tell you if I were?"

The dark girl nodded slowly. "Yes, I believe you would. I don't like you. I think you came here to try and marry Quentin. But I do feel you are a completely honest person."

"Well, that's something," Lara said with a bitter smile.

"And I think you've seen enough and heard enough since you've come to Collinwood to make you change your mind about wanting to become Quentin's wife. I'd just like to have you honestly tell me if that's so."

"Suppose I can't?"

"I think you can if you want to," Catherine said. She hesitated. "A great deal may depend on it."

"After the way you've behaved toward me you're asking quite a lot."

Catherine's lovely face was deathly pale. "It will be to your advantage to tell me. Unless you don't mind dying the way that Mary did."

The words hit Lara with a frightening impact. "What do you mean?"

"I can't explain yet," the other girl said. "Not until I'm sure how you feel about Quentin."

"You're saying that Quentin killed Mary?"

"I'm not saying anything until I hear from you," Catherine said firmly.

Lara began to feel that Catherine knew Quentin's secret: that he suffered under the curse of the werewolf and in his animal form had torn open his wife's throat. And she couldn't understand the girl's continued love for him. But then, love was a force no one could explain. It was almost a rule that it continued to thrive despite tragedy and disillusionment. She decided it might be best to tell this unhappy girl truly how she felt. "Very well. I'm not in love with Quentin."

Catherine brightened. "You aren't?" And then at once she became suspicious again. "You'd tell me that anyway."

"No," Lara said. "I'm being honest. It's possible I did arrive here with some romantic notions about Quentin. He and my father had written to each other for years. He loves my father's music. But as soon as I met. . . . any case, there is someone else."

"I see," Catherine said. "Is it Conrad?"

"I didn't agree to tell you that," Lara said easily. "I've already told you what you wanted to know."

Catherine was staring at her and suddenly her eyes opened wide. "Now I think I know who it is! Barnabas!"

Lara couldn't hold back the rush of crimson to her cheeks. "I don't want to discuss it. I want you to tell me if Quentin killed his wife."

The dark girl looked uneasy. "I know how it happened," she said. "And I'm going to make sure it doesn't happen to you. That's all I can tell you."

"You're not keeping your part of the bargain," Lara accused her.

But Catherine was already on her way to the hall door. She

paused with her hand on the knob to tell Lara over her shoulder. "You keep your word and I'll keep mine. Remember what I told you." When she opened the door she peered out into the corridor as if to make sure no one was watching, and then hurried on her way, closing the door after her.

It had been a completely unexpected confrontation. Coming on the heels of the macabre scene with Quentin below, it left Lara feeling dizzy. Things were beginning to happen at a rapid pace. In spite of herself, she had the feeling that Catherine meant what she said.

Suddenly she thought she heard a rush of footsteps and a gasping in the hall outside. Icy fear at once cut through her. She glanced toward the door with widened eyes, wondering what it might mean. It could be nothing more than one of the maids running upstairs to her room or it could be another dread happening in this house of tragedy.

She waited for long minutes and there was only silence. Her fear abating, she went across to the door and opened it, staring out into the shadows of the hall. But the shadows revealed no one. And then, just as she was about to go back into her room, she thought she saw something move at the very end of the corridor. For just an instant she had a vision of burning animal eyes and a crouched wolf-like form. Then the form dissolved in the shadows and she knew that it had been an illusion, a trick her imagination had played on her. With a sigh she went back into her room and bolted the door.

The first night in her new bedroom passed without any further disturbances. She did not hear Quentin come up to his adjoining room or any other sounds. When she awoke, a gray morning light was shining in through the slit between her window drapes. She guessed that the new day was not a fine one. And by the time she was up and dressed this was confirmed. It was not raining, but a heavy fog shut off the view of the bay altogether. She could not see beyond the cliff's edge.

Not inexplicably she found herself in a depressed mood. The dreadful scene with Quentin the previous night had shocked her. He had seemed in agony when he'd staggered off down the hall and vanished into the study. She wondered if this had been a prelude to his transforming into an animal form or if it had signified some other kind of attack. She couldn't help wondering whether he'd be at the dining table when she went down for breakfast.

It wasn't Quentin who greeted her at the table but Conrad. The quiet younger brother stood and smiled as she joined him for the meal. While the maid waited on her Lara questioned him.

"Has Quentin been down for breakfast?"

Conrad said, "No. He's ill this morning. He's having his breakfast in his room."

"I see."

Conrad sipped his coffee. "I don't think he had much sleep last night. He had another of his spells and was out most of the night wandering around. When the pain hits him he claims he can't rest."

"That's too bad," she said, putting sugar on her oatmeal. Had he prowled the estate the previous night as a werewolf?

"If he keeps on he'll be getting as bad a reputation as Barnabas," Conrad said with a smile Lara found annoyingly insolent.

"I wasn't aware that Barnabas had all that bad a reputation."

"Pretty grim," Conrad assured her. "About half the folks in the village claim he's a vampire."

"But that's ridiculous," she said sharply.

Conrad's pleasant face showed amused resignation. "I wouldn't dare offer an opinion. I don't know about you."

"He is your cousin. You should protect his reputation."

"He should do that himself. This thing he has about appearing only at night is bad enough. But on top of that he's always seeking out village girls on lonely roads and dazzling them with his talk. And when he's not making enemies by doing that he's giving people nervous scares by wandering around in cemeteries after dark."

"None of those things mean he's abnormal."

"They add up to something not too pleasant. The Collinsport people remember that the first Barnabas Collins was a pretty strange character."

"It's unfair to link Barnabas with a man dead for nearly two hundred years!"

Conrad shrugged. "That's the kind of people they are."

"I hate small towns."

He studied her with mocking eyes. "Then you wouldn't ever think about living here?"

"No."

He sighed. "I've grown to like it. And of course it's an ideal spot for my dogs."

She looked up from her oatmeal, which, she reflected, she had never liked. "You're very devoted to them, aren't you?"

"Major thing in my life."

"I admire that," she said. "But I am terrified of the dogs. I believe your training of them is too rough. You've turned them into cruel creatures."

"Just into good watch dogs," he amended her. "The rest of the time they're gentle as kittens."

Before she could make any comment, a blood-curdling series of screams rang out from somewhere upstairs!

CHAPTER 8

Lara and Conrad looked at each other for a frozen instant, then jumped up from the table with Conrad awkwardly leading the way out of the dining room. The eerie wailing went on.

As they started up the stairs Conrad shouted back over his shoulder, "Sounds like Aunt Erica. The old girl may have finally lost her mind altogether. I hope she hasn't harmed Catherine."

"I hope not," Lara said breathlessly as she went up the stairs a step behind him.

She did not know what the terrible cries meant but she had the dread suspicion this was the answer to her mood of depression. She had somehow sensed impending tragedy. Now they were caught up in the crisis of it.

The wailing which had changed into a kind of sobbing, was plainly coming from the third floor.

In spite of his crippled foot Conrad made excellent progress up the stairs and was the first to reach the distraught old woman. Wearing a tattered robe, Erica leaned weakly against the newel post, clutching it with an emaciated claw. Her thinning white hair was uncombed and wildly askew while her pinched, wrinkled face wore a look of pained incredulity.

Reaching her, Conrad grasped her by the arm and demanded, "What's wrong with you, old woman?"

Aunt Erica ceased her keening and gave him a stunned look. "The demons!" she croaked.

Conrad continued to hold onto her and as Lara reached the landing gave her a significant glance. "I guess it's finally happened. Quentin said she should be in an asylum."

"But where's Catherine?" Lara asked. "She's always with her."

Looking concerned, he turned to Erica. "Where is Catherine?"

The old woman tried to pull away from him with a frightened expression on her thin, parchment face. "The Devil's own!" she said hoarsely.

"We'll go find her," Conrad said. And he swung the weak old creature around with ease. But at once Aunt Erica drew back with wild cries of fear.

Lara cried, "Don't try to force her! She'll be hurt!"

"I can't let her behave in this fashion!" Conrad exclaimed in disgust. But he did let the old woman free and she at once collapsed limply against the corridor wall, moaning.

Conrad went striding down the hall with Lara hurrying after him. The door to Aunt Erica's apartment was open. Through it they saw the motionless figure of Catherine sprawled out on the floor. Conrad muttered an oath and came to a halt, then turned quickly to prevent Lara from seeing what he had just witnessed. But he hadn't moved quickly enough to stop her from getting a brief glimpse of the girl's distorted features and torn, bloody throat.

"On, no!" she groaned as she allowed Conrad to take her in his arms and prevent her from fainting.

"Don't think about it," he counseled her. "We have things to do."

"Her throat!" Lara said weakly. "How?"

"Looks like the same thing that happened to Mary," Conrad said grimly. "Someone or something murdered Catherine by tearing her throat open."

"I saw her late last night," Lara said. "And then I thought I heard a scuffling noise in the hall."

"You saw her? Where?"

"She came to my room. She said she knew who murdered Mary."

Conrad stared at her. "Did she say who?"

Lara found herself in a dreadful dilemma. Catherine had strongly hinted that Quentin was the killer, Quentin in his role of werewolf. But she dared not make this accusation on the flimsy evidence she possessed. She would have to allow the authorities to solve it for themselves. But this shouldn't be too difficult since this was the second such murder on the estate.

Conrad shook her. "You haven't answered me!"

"She didn't say who," Lara managed. "She didn't tell me."

"I thought you would have something to help," Conrad said

with disgust. "We'll have to let Quentin know and then inform the local police. And somebody will have to look after Aunt Erica."

By the time they reached the old woman again, the housekeeper was with her, and at Conrad's direction took Erica to her own room to look after her until some order was restored in the house.

Going downstairs, they came face to face with a pale and abject Quentin on the first landing. The young man was wearing a velvet dressing gown tied at the waist with a golden cord. He smoothed back his mass of slightly curly hair and stared at them with troubled, questioning eyes.

"What is it?"

Conrad looked at him so coldly that Lara was sure he had guessed Quentin's awful secret. He said, "It's Catherine! Someone killed her up in Erica's apartment. Tore her throat open just as they did Mary's."

"One of the dogs!" Quentin cried in horror.

Conrad at once seized him by the front of the crimson robe and glowered at him as he shouted back, "I'll have none of that this time. You tried to put it off on my dogs before. It didn't work even then. Mary's body was found on the beach but Catherine is up there on the third floor! Are you going to say a dog found its way up there and did it?"

"It's not impossible!"

"So near it that it doesn't matter," Conrad said grimly, releasing his brother's robe. "Besides, none of my animals were out of the kennel last night. I'll swear to that!"

Quentin was caught between anger and despair. "You'd swear to anything to protect those crazy beasts!" And he swung around to her. "What do you know about this, Lara?"

He looked as if he might collapse at any moment. Lara couldn't help wondering if this was a case of fear or of guilty conscience. The vision of the moment when he'd suffered that agonizing spell haunted her.

"I know very little about it," she said in a small voice. "I saw her up there just now. And after I talked to you I saw her for a few minutes in my room last night."

Quentin frowned. "Why did she visit you? You weren't friends."

"She seemed to suddenly want to make up for our quarrel," Lara said.

Conrad spoke up angrily. "You're wasting time asking her questions. I've already talked to her about it. She hasn't any help to offer."

Quentin glanced at her. "Is that true?"

"Yes," she said, feeling ill. "It was a personal visit. Just a girl-to-girl talk without any bearing on what happened to her."

"I see," Quentin said grimly.

"May I go to my room?" she asked. "I feel ill."

"I'll see you safely there," Conrad said, and he escorted her down the hall to her door. He was proving the better man in this crisis.

Lara remained in her room for several hours after that. Someone sent one of the young maids to sit with her – a needless gesture, Lara thought. But she didn't insist the girl leave. She let her remain, though she refused to talk with her. So the uneasy maid sat dumbly by, a silent sentinel.

Lara had plenty to occupy her thoughts. She had no doubt that when Quentin suffered his spell downstairs it had been the beginning of his transformation into a werewolf. Later, a vicious, fanged animal, he had lurked in the corridor shadows for Catherine and then followed her up to the apartment. There he had pounced on her and ripped open her throat.

But did he have any remembrance of doing it? Or had he just learned of his monstrous act when they met him in the hall? Even Barnabas hadn't been sure about that. She longed to be able to see him, hear his views, rely on his moral support. But she couldn't expect to see Barnabas until dusk. No matter what the emergency he never broke that rule of not appearing until after sundown.

So she would wait. In the meantime the police chief arrived. She heard the heavy steps in the hall and on the stairs and wondered how it would all turn out. How Quentin would emerge from this? What would they do? Treat him like a madman? And if they did place him in some institution, could he be confined successfully? Or would he, some night when the moon was full or the evil rose up in him, assume the greenish-gray wolf form again to prowl and kill?

If the murders were calculated, he had likely murdered Mary because she'd discovered what he'd become. And he'd killed Catherine because he guessed she was either about to inform on him or blackmail him into marrying her and reforming. Quentin might have been willing to make amends, but under the spell it would be the beast poor Catherine would have had to deal with. And of course the beast would be merciless.

The day continued foggy and gloomy. The little maid assigned to her went down and brought her some broth and crackers for lunch. She barely managed to get these down. The tension of what was going on around her and the horror of what she had seen on the third floor had shattered her.

It was mid-afternoon when Quentin came to her room with the law officer. Quentin was all serenity now, though pale. He wore his usual smartly-cut dark suit along with his regular winged collar and fawn cravat. All the indecision and fear he'd shown earlier had vanished.

"This gentleman wishes to question you," he told her.

"Very well," she said.

The maid was sent from the room and while Quentin stood by, silent and weary-looking, the police chief proceeded to ask Lara a series of questions. He was an elderly man in shabby clothing and did not strike her as too bright. In fact, he didn't even appear much interested in what had happened.

He seemed to be chiefly concerned about finding some witness to the murder. "You didn't hear any familiar voices or see anyone after Miss Edmonds left you?"

Seated in a rocking chair by the window, Lara considered. "Not really. I thought I heard a funny scuffling noise once. And when I looked out I had a moment when I was sure I saw a giant animal at the far end of the corridor. It looked like a wolf with burning eyes. And then it just vanished and I knew it must have been my imagination."

He fingered his greasy felt hat nervously. "As I understand it, you thought you saw a dog, miss?"

"No." She denied this at once. "It looked like a wolf. But it wasn't anything. I realized it was an illusion."

"But just suppose you were right the first time and it was a dog," the policeman said with too eager interest and ignoring her denial. He turned to Quentin and told him, "This young lady's statement bears out my theory about the dogs. I say one of them somehow escaped the kennel last night and got into the house and upstairs. There would be lots of chances for it. He caught that girl as she was going into the apartment and made short work of her. The scuffling sound would have been him going upstairs."

Quentin nodded savagely. "I think you're right," he said. "It's the same story as with Mary. Those dogs have been a curse. But I doubt if you'll get my brother to do away with them."

The old man spread his hands. "In that case I won't be responsible for anything else that happens here. The blood will be on his hands." He gave Lara a genial nod. "Thank you, miss," he said. "You've been a great help." And he left the room.

Quentin lingered behind to offer her a sad smile. "It was good of you to see him, Lara. Every detail is important."

She had gotten to her feet impatiently. "But he has it all wrong. I didn't tell him it was the dogs who were responsible. He's putting words into my mouth."

"Likely the proper words," Quentin suggested.

"Nonsense," she protested. "How could a dog get in the house? That kills the theory in the first place."

Quentin looked almost smug. "I regret to tell you one of the side doors was left a trifle ajar. We found it that way this morning. Any animal, wild or domestic, could have made its way in and through the corridors to the main section of the house."

"I'm sure it wasn't the dogs," she argued. "I've never said anything else. But I suppose Conrad will think I have and hate me. You're being too unfair to him."

"I fear you're badly confused," was Quentin's quiet comment. He went out and left her standing there thoroughly frustrated.

It was as if a wall was being erected around her. Quentin had cleverly managed things to divert the suspicion from himself and make Conrad's dogs seem the villains of the situation. Of course Conrad would argue none of the dogs were free to commit the crime and Quentin would claim his crippled brother was merely covering up for the dogs to protect them.

She could even picture them bringing in the possibility that a wild dog or a stray wolf had somehow gotten into the house. The truth was too completely bizarre! Who would listen to a theory suggesting that something had happened to make Quentin turn into a werewolf at certain times? And it was he who was doing these killings while under the spell. The fat police chief wouldn't ever credit such a story!

Yet everyone knew that Collinwood was a place of weird happenings. And they hadn't hesitated to accuse Barnabas of being one of the living dead. Why should they insist that the deaths of Mary and Catherine had come about through purely normal circumstances? Why rule out the supernatural? And then a new worry crossed her mind.

If she complained and finally got them thinking her way, the finger of suspicion might be pointed at Barnabas rather than Quentin. They already had wild ideas that Barnabas was a vampire maintaining life by robbing young women of blood. It wouldn't need too much stretching of imagination to make it seem likely he was also the one who'd turned to tearing open throats. This frightening possibility completed her frustration.

It seemed she would have to allow Conrad to think she had betrayed him and go on hating her. She couldn't come out with the werewolf story without placing Barnabas in danger. And she would not do that!

A glance at the pale little maid who had returned served to make her doubly angry. She couldn't go on in this grim charade. She felt a deep need to leave the house. Even though it was damp and foggy outside, she had to get some air and think away from the grim walls of the old mansion.

Hastily donning a cloak, she left the room. She went straight downstairs and out, not hesitating to give anyone a chance to note her leaving and make a protest. Stepping out into the damp mist, she felt better. The gray afternoon was heralding the approach of evening; she would soon be able to see Barnabas and he would help her.

The grass of the lawn was glistening and wet. The moisture went through her slippers but she paid no attention to it. She wanted to put a distance between her and the dark old mansion. She made her way to the edge of the cliff and stood for a moment listening to the ghostly wash of the waves she couldn't see because of the fog. From Collinsport Point the foghorn was giving out its monotonous regular blast of warning. Melancholy seemed to have closed in on all the world.

A bit further on, she found a path that led rather precariously down the face of the steep cliff. Carefully picking her steps, she descended the path until she reached the sand and rocks of the shore. The tide was just beginning to turn and there was still a fairly wide expanse of beach.

Just being out of the house and by herself helped. But she was still beset by the dilemma of what to do. It wasn't right that these murders should go unavenged. Nor was it right to allow Quentin to continue killing. But how to stop him?

She jumped as a rock bounced off a boulder near her. And then she stood stock still with growing fear as she realized someone must have thrown the rock in her path, perhaps preparing for some other more direct assault on her. She waited with bated breath.

From the boulders above there was the sound of movement and a familiar voice called out, "I didn't mean to make your heart stop beating. Only wanted to attract your attention."

She looked up and saw the young man in the dark plaid suit and cap standing on a rocky plateau above her. "It's you!"

"Michael Green," he said in his brash, friendly way. "You have to remember me. Last time your friend put his dog on me."

"I remember," she said. "I begged him not to do it."

"Now that was very nice of you, Miss Balfour," the young man said and with amazing agility quickly clambered down from the boulders to stand beside her.

"You seem to enjoy scaring me," she said. "Last time it was in the cemetery."

The young man looked embarrassed. "I don't mean to. It's just my way. I wanted to catch your attention without doing a lot of shouting. I have an idea the Collins family would still think of me as a trespasser, even down here."

"I imagine so."

"And I really came along the beach in the hope of meeting you."

She regarded him with some skepticism. "I doubt that."

"I mean it," he said, becoming serious. "I want to talk to you about the murder at Collinwood."

Lara was startled. "You know so soon?"

"It's all around the village."

"But how can they say that it's a murder?" she asked.

The young man looked grim. "It happened at Collinwood. Isn't that enough? And how many young women just accidentally fall and rip their throats open? It has to be murder."

"The police chief seems to believe one of Conrad's dogs did it," she said bitterly.

Michael Green's mouth dropped open. "Not again. That's how they got away with it last time. But I hear the body of Miss Edmonds was found upstairs in the house. How could a dog get up there?"

"A side door was conveniently left open by someone last night," she said with irony.

The young man shook his head in despair. "I might have guessed it."

"So an animal, wild or domestic, could have entered the house."

His sharp eyes met hers. "Do you think that's what happened? I mean honestly think so?"

"No."

"Nor do I," he said angrily. "As I've suspected this was all carefully planned in advance."

There was an authority in the young man's manner she couldn't ignore. Looking hard at him, she asked, "How can you know so much about it?"

"I've made a study of Mary Collins' murder."

Her eyes opened wide, "But why?"

He glanced around the fog-ridden beach rather apprehensively. Even looking up at the edge of the cliff barely visible in the thick mist above them. Then he gave his attention to her.

"No one followed you, did they?"

"I think not. Why do you ask?"

"I'm not anxious to be discovered here at this time," he said. "And it mightn't be the best thing for you. I mean being seen with me."

"What are you talking about?"

Michael Green's pleasant face was earnest. "You must accept that you're dealing with a murderer. Someone who will show you no more mercy than he has the others if he comes to believe you are aligned against him."

Lara stared at him. "Just how much do you know?"

"Enough."

"How much is enough?" She stood there in the swirling mist with the cloak wrapped tightly around her. She was positive Michael Green had something to contribute to the mystery if only he deigned to confide in her.

He took her by the arm. "Let us walk a bit," he said. "I have the uneasy feeling that we might be overheard here."

"I doubt it," she said. "The sound of the waves must cover our voices."

"Just the same," he urged her. And she allowed him to lead her closer to the water on the part of the beach where there was a fairly wide expanse of sand. They strolled along for perhaps fifty yards before coming to a place where the overhang of the cliffs made an inviting place of concealment. There he took her over to stand close to the damp face of the cliff with him. In this spot there was no danger of their being seen.

She was beginning to be wary of him. After all, he was a complete stranger except for the chance encounter they had in the cemetery. And both of their meetings had come about under rather strange circumstances. Who could this man be? And what did he want at Collinwood?

She said, "You're very particular about a place to talk."

"Yes," he said dryly.

"I know nothing about you," she reminded him. "You might even be the one who murdered Mary and Catherine, since you seem to know so much about what happened to them."

His eyes met hers. "An interesting idea. Do you really take it seriously?"

Alone with him in this isolated area of the deserted beach she was beginning to feel a little afraid. But she wasn't anxious to let him be aware of it, even though she'd brought up the subject of not really knowing anything about him.

Pretending to be casual, she said, "I'm merely pointing out that you're expecting me to have a lot of faith in you and your stories."

"I suppose I am."

"A wiser girl than I likely wouldn't have let you entice her here like this, a distance away from everyone. If I screamed, I'd be lucky if I was heard."

He nodded significantly. "That's true."

Lara was puzzled by the strength of his personality. This seemingly casual young man had a way of suddenly becoming persuasive and firm. There was a strangeness in him she had not fathomed.

She said, "What is it you want to tell me?"

"Let me ask you a question first."

"Well?"

He was staring at her hard. "Do you believe there are such things as werewolves?"

She shrugged. "I've never given it any thought. It sounds fantastic."

"The villagers here in Collinsport don't think so. They believe there is a werewolf preying on the area. And werewolves abound in the folklore of nearly every country. The legend is widespread."

"Why are you telling me this?"

He smiled thinly. "Because I believe your host at Collinwood, Quentin Collins, is a werewolf. There is a story in the village that he was cursed by a gypsy. Probably you've heard it."

"No, I haven't."

"The transformation of a man into a wolf is known as lycanthropy. I have an idea the old woman Erica could tell you all about it. She is generally regarded as a witch."

"That's because she is very old and demented and strange looking."

"In her younger days she was active as the leader of a Satanist circle," Michael Green informed her. "I think she may have been the first to interest Quentin in the supernatural."

"And you think that Quentin assumed the form of a wolf and did the murders?"

"Yes," he said. "I'll not accept stories of wandering mad dogs or stray wolves as the killers. Nor do I believe that any of Conrad Collins' dogs escaped from their kennels to commit the crimes."

"You prefer the supernatural explanation."

"Yes."

"I'd hardly expect that from you," she said, searching his plain but pleasant face for some clue to what he was thinking.

"I have my mystical side."

"Why are you interested in what has happened here at all?" she asked. "You're only a visitor, a stranger supposedly here in the village for your health."

"Curiosity is a universal thing."

"But such a special kind of curiosity," she insisted. "I've often wondered what you were searching for in the cemetery?"

"In that case I wasn't searching for anything. I was merely looking around." He paused. "I was also hoping I might encounter the mysterious Barnabas Collins."

"Why would you want to meet him?" she asked uneasily.

"Because he offers another explanation of the murders. The villagers are as afraid of him as they are of Quentin. They claim Barnabas is mad. The killings would appear to be the work of a madman."

"It could be Quentin who is mad," she said. "He might have insane spells and consider himself an avenging animal."

Michael Green studied her with fresh interest. "Smart young woman," he said. "I've thought of that myself."

"So there are many possibilities."

"Indeed there are," he agreed. "I'm puzzled that you don't leave Collinwood at once."

"I have good reasons for remaining."

"I hope you're not in love with Quentin."

Lara was about to tell him of how Catherine had questioned her in the same vein before her murder, but she didn't get the chance. At that instant there was an ominous rumble from above and hard on its heels a veritable landslide came down on them. She screamed as Michael Green protectively took a stand in front of her to try and save her from the loose earth and heavy rocks.

CHAPTER 9

The dangerous rain of earth and rocks went on for several minutes. When it eased to a dribble, all around them was a barrier of fallen rocks left by the sudden landslide. Lara's cloak was a mess from streaks of the muddy earth as was Michael's suit and cap.

He gasped. "That was a close one!"

She nodded. "If we hadn't been protected by the overhang we'd have been killed."

He still made no attempt to move but tried to brush some of the dirt from him as he took note of the pile of rubble all about them. "It was a near thing at that."

She shook some of the soft earth from her cloak. "What could have started it?"

He gave her a wise glance. "Or who?"

"Who?"

"Yes," he said grimly. "Somebody up on the cliffs may have seen us come to this spot. Then they made their way to the cliff's edge above us and loosened the gravel enough to get this going."

"I don't believe that."

"You think it was just coincidence?"

"Yes."

"I'd like to be as sure," he told her with skepticism. "Right now I'm most anxious to get out of here." And he cautiously emerged from their place of safety and clambered over the high mound of earth and rocks. Then he turned and held out his hand to help her mount the uneven heap and escape to the open beach.

He said, "We'd better go our separate ways. I still think that landslide was arranged for our benefit."

"In that case whoever went to the trouble failed miserably," she told him with a bleak smile.

He stared back at the spot thoughtfully. "Of course, they'll make another try."

"You think so?"

"Bound to."

"Before we leave," she said, "why don't you tell me something more about yourself?"

He looked at her with ironic amusement. "Are you showing a personal interest in me suddenly?"

She blushed. "You know what I mean."

"I'm actually a very dull character," he said. "But I'll lead you on for my own selfish reasons. To make sure of seeing you again. If you'll meet me at the cemetery early tomorrow evening I'll give you my history."

"What time?"

"Any time between seven and eight," he told her. "And I may have some startling things to tell you about the murders as well."

She frowned. "Now you're talking in riddles again."

"Wait until tomorrow," he said. "In the meantime I'll see you safely up to the cliff top."

They left the fog-ridden beach and went up the path to the level of the cliffs. He remained there only a moment to say goodbye to her and then vanished down the path again, disappearing in the fog. She watched him go with mingled emotions.

How had he learned so much about Collinwood and its people? And why was he forever lurking on the grounds of the estate? He had to have more than an ordinary interest in what was happening. Perhaps if she met him tomorrow she would at last learn some of the answers.

As she turned to walk toward the house, the foghorn out on the point kept up its melancholy wailing. She moved slowly through the wraithlike mist, deep in solemn thought. The horror of the discovery of Catherine's mutilated body was still with her. And she was almost certain the lovely dark girl had died because she'd learned Quentin's dread secret.

Collinwood was still hidden by the mists as she walked on across the lawn. And then to her right a figure suddenly showed like an emerging ghost. It was Conrad Collins with Caesar on a leash. The giant dog saw her and began barking and straining at the leash. Conrad spoke angrily to the beast and yanked him back. The immediate result was a low snarling from Caesar but he calmed down.

Conrad continued toward her with the big gray dog. "You needn't be afraid," he said. "Caesar recognizes you now."

"He has a fearsome bark."

Conrad halted a few feet from her, keeping the uneasy dog on a tight rein. "He's perfectly harmless. The best trained of all my dogs. Quentin is the only one who considers him a menace."

"Because of what happened," she suggested.

"No dog could have gotten into the house and killed Catherine that way and escaped again," Conrad said bitterly. "Quentin is drawing on his imagination. The alibi fitted in a sort of way when Mary was killed. But not this time."

"The door was open," she reminded him. "An animal could have gotten inside."

"Or a human," Conrad said, his eyes fixed directly on her. "Have you considered that?"

"Truthfully, I hadn't," she admitted. She had no intention of bringing her suspicions of Quentin into this conversation with his brother. So she went on to say, "Perhaps because of the manner of her murder. I mean the horrible way her throat was ripped open. Surely only an animal could be capable of that."

Caesar was pulling at his leash and whimpering. His odd amber eyes were staring at Lara. Conrad gave the big gray dog a slap and sternly ordered him to be silent once again. Then he told Lara, "I wouldn't jump to that conclusion. A human could do the same kind of damage with some sort of rough weapon and make it look like the work of an animal's fangs."

"Who would want to kill Catherine?"

"I've been thinking of someone," he said. "What about that fellow we found in the cemetery the other day?"

"Michael Green?"

"I guess that was his name. What is he doing around here? He didn't seem to be able to give any satisfactory answer. I'd say he's some kind of crazy person. And Catherine's murder seemed like a lunatic's work. For all we know the same fellow may have been in the area when Mary was killed and committed that crime as well."

"I'm sure you're wrong," she protested.

"How can you be sure?"

She hesitated. "Because I've found him very nice. I don't think he'd be capable of anything like that."

"That's what you want to think," Conrad said in an icy manner. "Just as Quentin closes his eyes to every possible suspect but my dogs."

Lara said, "I do want to be fair. But you have no reason to suspect a young man like Michael Green. It's too farfetched."

"How can you say that? You don't really know anything about him."

"I trust my impression of him."

"And you could be very wrong!"

"I could be. I don't think I am."

"If Quentin makes any more accusations against my dogs I'm going to bring this Green fellow into it whether you like it or not," Conrad said.

She raised her eyebrows. "So that's why you've decided to involve an innocent young man. To clear your dogs of any blame."

"I know my dogs."

"I hope so."

"And I'll not get rid of them for Quentin or the police chief or anyone else," Conrad assured her angrily. "I've always thought of you as my friend but you're letting me down in this."

She kept the cloak tightly around her to protect her from the cool damp air. "I haven't meant to," she said unhappily.

"Everyone is against me," Conrad went on. "But I'll not give in. I'll defend my dogs to the last."

"If none of them are guilty I certainly wouldn't want to blame them," Lara assured him. "I like dogs. I had one of my own when my father was alive."

Caesar tugged at the leash and gave a short bark. Conrad reproved him again and studied her with fresh interest. "You've never told me that before. What kind of dog was it?"

"A basset hound," she said. "I had to give him away when I moved."

"You must have missed him," Conrad said.

"I did."

He turned frowning in the direction of the house. "Quentin has never wanted me to have the kennel. It was bad enough when Mary was killed but he's going to be worse now. But he won't get his way!"

"What if positive proof turns up it was one of your dogs?"

He glanced at her angrily. "That will never happen! Come, Caesar!" And he twisted the dog around and strode off into the mist again.

Lara found it hard to be unsympathetic towards the crippled young man, yet she thought he was being as unreasonable as anyone in refusing to believe his dogs could be guilty. He had good reason for his angry defense of them if he knew about the werewolf curse which was on Quentin. But if this was so, why not denounce his brother rather than shift the blame to an innocent like Michael Green?

She could think of several reasons. Perhaps Conrad balked at revealing the truth about his brother to the authorities even if they didn't get on well. There was the tie of blood between them. And as far as Conrad was concerned, Michael Green was an intruding stranger who might even be a criminal. To point a finger of suspicion his way was a logical move.

With this realization she continued on to Collinwood. There was no one around when she entered the grim old mansion. She went upstairs, keenly aware of the deathly silence of the house which had so recently been the scene of a murder. Letting herself into her room, she was about to cross to her dresser when she glanced at the bed and screamed.

Neatly placed on the center of the white bedspread was what seemed like a tiny dead mouse. And around it someone had drawn a circle in blood or some other red liquid. At once she thought of the mad old Erica and looked wildly about the room, but could see no one. She took a step nearer the bed and peering at the odious object saw that it wasn't a mouse but a small bat.

Wearily rubbing the back of her hand across her forehead, she stood there debating what she would do. She decided to quickly change into the dress she'd wear for the evening and go down and tell Quentin.

Avoiding the ugly thing on the bed she went across to her closet. As she took the green dress from the rack she made another startling discovery. Many of her dresses had been taken from their hangers and thrown on the floor. And the green dress in her hand had been marked insanely with a series of crimson crosses in a liquid similar to that used to make the weird circle on the bed. It was too much!

She was still standing there staring dazedly at the dress when she heard the cackling laughter from a distance across the room. She wheeled around to see Aunt Erica standing there. The pinched face of the crone showed delight and she pointed a bony forefinger at her.

"The Devil is in your body!" the old woman croaked. "And Catherine's throat was opened to the sunlight!"

She strode angrily across to face the old woman with the ruined dress held up for her to see. "Why did you do this spiteful thing?"

Erica's sunken, rheumy eyes glittered madly. "The bat will settle with you. The bat will level you with the others. Your blood will vanish and your white face with sightless eyes will stare up at the sunrise!"

Disgusted and terrified, Lara stood there helplessly listening to the insane gibberish. Fortunately at that moment the housekeeper who had been assigned to take care of the madwoman appeared in the doorway behind Erica.

"You wicked old woman!" the housekeeper scolded her. "I've been searching for you for more than an hour! How dare you leave your apartment. You know Mr. Quentin won't have it!" She gave Lara an apologetic glance. "I hope she hasn't bothered you too much!" And with that she grasped Erica's arm and dragged her protesting from the room.

Lara stood there stunned for a few seconds. Then she wearily turned and went back to the closet and began to take stock of her wardrobe. Three of her best dresses were stained and ruined. She set them aside and hung the others up. When this was done she took the bedspread from her bed, carefully folding it with the dead bat left in it and set it on the floor for the maid to take away. Then she dressed to go down to dinner.

Ill with indignation at this latest invasion of her privacy, she felt little like eating. She intended to tell Quentin about it though she expected him to do nothing. He was in too troubled a state of mind concerning himself to take much interest in the problems of others.

As she put the finishing touches to her upswept hair before the dresser mirror she wondered whether the professed witch, Aunt Erica, could have had any part in the two murders. In her younger days she had predicted the deaths of many and been active in witchcraft. Did she have the power to become a snarling animal and tear open throats?

The idea was too repulsive. Lara tried to blot it from her mind. When she went downstairs and entered the living room she was surprised to find Quentin there by himself with the gramophone playing her father's waltz. It ended just as she came up by the master of Collinwood.

Quentin bowed to her. "I suppose you think it heartless of me to be enjoying your father's music with Catherine only a few hours dead. But this was not meant in disrespect. I was thinking of her as the music went on."

"I understand," she said quietly.

"What a dreadful business it is," Quentin lamented, looking his usual gentlemanly self in winged collar and dark suit. "I shall never rest until I find out the truth about her murder."

"That may be difficult." She feared that Quentin had no memory of the crimes he'd committed in his werewolf form. What would be his reaction when he found out?

"The funeral will be in the old cemetery tomorrow afternoon," Quentin told her. "I'll be happy to have you attend. It will be a private affair confined to the family."

"Has the police chief come up with any new clues to the murderer?"

Quentin held his hands straight at his sides and was now opening and closing them in an unconscious gesture of uneasiness. "No. I think not. My brother has mentioned a stranger who has been lurking on the estate but I still believe it was one of the dogs." As he spoke she saw that his right hand was still bandaged as it had been since the night Barnabas had fired a shot into the snarling beast's right paw and it ran off howling.

"Everything points to some kind of animal."

Quentin gave her a sharp glance. "Yes, I agree."

"Will Barnabas be invited to the funeral?"

He furrowed his brow. "I'll let his man know if I don't see him before the funeral. It will be at four so I doubt if he'll break his work routine to be there."

"That doesn't sound like Barnabas," she said. "He's such a sincere person."

Quentin smiled coldly. "I fear you are still ignorant of the true nature of my cousin. I have had so many complaints about his odd behavior from the villagers that I'm going to be forced at last to ask him to leave."

"Please, don't do that," she begged. "The local people are being unreasonable because they don't understand him."

Quentin compressed his lips grimly. "I haven't the leisure to try and investigate their feelings in the matter," he said. "I feel I have no right to allow Barnabas to remain in the face of their objections."

She wanted to divert him before he announced the date when he wanted Barnabas to depart. So she at once launched into a dramatic account of the havoc Erica had wrought in her room. Quentin listened gravely as they stood there amid the luxurious surroundings in the glow of the soft light of the hanging crystal chandeliers. Outside the foghorn continued its dreary vigil as early darkness settled on the coastal village.

When Lara had finished her account of the old woman's depredations Quentin said, "Please accept my humblest apologies. When I asked you here I had no idea this unsettling series of events would take place."

Lara said, "Tragedy had already visited Collinwood in your wife's strange death. You didn't mention that in any of your letters."

"I was too depressed by it," Quentin said sadly, his eyes on his bandaged right hand for a moment. "Writing to you and your father helped preserve my sanity."

She nodded. "In all fairness I mustn't blame you for any predicament I may find myself in. You did send me that letter telling me not to come. It is unfortunate I didn't receive it."

"I have worried about that," he admitted. "But then I tell myself how thankful I am that you did come. You mustn't let Erica upset you. I'll see that your dresses are replaced. And I will take added precautions to keep her confined to her own part of the house."

"Even in her present state she is wily," Lara said. "I doubt if you will be able to manage her."

"Then she shall go to an institution. I have warned her."

"That does seem harsh."

"Not when I consider her actions towards you," Quentin said. "This house has seen enough trouble without her causing more."

"Thank you," she said.

"My own illness has left me weak and unable to cope with matters as I once did," Quentin worried. "My memory is uncertain. I have frightening blackouts."

She went tense. "Blackouts?"

He nodded gravely, his sensitive face showing his concern. "One moment I will be sitting at my desk. Then a seizure will hit me. The pain makes me forget everything else. And often when I come to myself it is minutes or even a half-hour later and I'm in another part of the house."

Lara frowned. "That is frightening. Have you had any medical advice?"

"No one seems to understand my case," he said. "If I continue to be plagued by my attacks I'm going to return to Boston for further talks with some of the outstanding medical men there."

"You should."

"I keep hoping they will go," he said with a sigh. "But then they return. I had one last night shortly before poor Catherine was murdered. When you discovered her body I was still ill and not able to comprehend all that was going on."

"Yes," she said, staring at him. "I thought you did seem strange."

"As soon as this is settled I'll go to Boston if the condition doesn't improve," Quentin assured her.

"You have no idea what you do in these blackouts?" she asked, searching his pale, troubled face.

"No," he said. "That's what frightens me. And I'm always weak and perspiring when I come to."

Lara decided he was either completely mad and unaware of it or a very convincing actor. He was becoming at times a werewolf without guessing what the seizures were, or else he was a kind of monster glorying in his evil and cannily providing himself with an alibi.

She said, "It is a very strange illness."

"You have helped me," he said in a gentle tone as he took her hand in his. "I have told you that I am in love with you."

"This is not the time to discuss it," she said uneasily.

"I realize that," he agreed. "Poor Catherine was so jealous of us. At least we do not have that to contend with now. But I would gladly suffer it if she could be returned to us alive."

"Please, I'd rather not talk of such things." She tried to draw her hand away but he held it.

"If I can rid myself of this dread illness you will marry me, won't you?" Quentin begged.

It was a difficult moment for her. She bit her lip and then said, "I think we should wait to go into that when you have had the verdict of the Boston doctors."

"Of course, you are right, dear Lara," he said, touching his lips to her forehead. Then Conrad joined them and they all went in to dinner. It was a sorry affair with little conversation and the ghost of Catherine shadowing the table.

She left the two men as soon as she gracefully could. Going to the window in the hall, she saw that darkness had come early. This meant she could go for a meeting with Barnabas at once. Not wanting to attract attention to her departure she went quietly upstairs to her room. She paced back and forth there for a little, thinking about it all.

The maid had come and turned down her bed; the bedspread with its hateful defilement had been taken away. Quentin's confession about his blackouts had fitted in with all her ideas concerning his state. If, as he contended, he had no memory of his actions while under the werewolf curse, it was possible for him to do any horrible thing and consider himself guiltless.

She was sure Barnabas would have something to add to the information she'd gained. He had spoken of making a series of inquiries in the village. She had not seen him since Catherine's murder and there was so much for them to discuss.

She went to the window and pulled back the drapes to stare out into the foggy night. A tall figure with a lantern was walking across the lawn in the direction of the barns. It was Conrad Collins on his nightly visit to the kennels. She could vaguely recognize him in the glow of the red lantern, but the loping walk of the crippled man was unmistakable.

A strange expression came over her attractive face. She found Conrad's affection for the savage animals in the kennel touching. He had claimed they meant more to him than any humans; she was ready to believe it. Once he had awkwardly reached out to show some affection for her but she had repulsed him. She feared he'd misunderstood her action and put it down to a dislike for him.

The truth was that among all the males at Collinwood only one stirred her heart – Barnabas. She only hoped that he would in turn come to love her. She had no doubt that he liked her. But he had maintained a certain aloofness between them that she didn't understand.

With a sigh she let the drapes close and went over to put on her cloak. The remaining stains of mud on it made her think of the afternoon and Michael Green. Even though she still didn't know much about him, she liked him. He had the same assurance and strength as Barnabas, in a different way. Again she wondered if that landslide had been purely accidental or a cleverly devised attempt to kill her and the stranger.

Quietly she went out into the hall and started down the stairs. She was on the way to the front door when Quentin appeared at the entrance to the living room, looking ill and hollow-eyed. And he stared at her in silence for seconds.

Then asked dully, "So you're going out?"

"Yes." She was embarrassed.

"On a night like this?"

"I thought I'd just go outside for the air," she faltered. "I have a headache."

"It is dark and foggy out there."

"I don't plan to stay long."

Quentin's eyes had taken on an odd glazed look. He said, "My head aches. I'm not well or I'd go along with you."

"I wouldn't want that," she said quickly. And then she realized she'd said it too quickly.

Even in his upset state the young master of Collinwood did not miss the uneasiness in her manner. "You're meeting someone, of course," he said bitterly.

"Not really."

"But you do hope to find Barnabas out there?"

"We sometimes meet when I'm having an evening walk," she admitted. She might as well. He'd already seen through her subterfuge.

"That's very convenient," he said with dull sarcasm. "Don't let me keep you." And he turned and went back into the living room.

Lara was distressed but there was nothing she could say. She went on out, unable to believe her bad luck in meeting him. It was colder outside and the heavy fog gave the darkness a menacing air. Holding the cloak close to her she began walking swiftly toward the old house.

She tried to bolster her courage with the thought that Barnabas might emerge from the ghostly mists at any moment. But he didn't. She continued on, worried about the scene with Quentin, aware that he had appeared on the verge of one of his transformations into the werewolf state.

And then she was suddenly aware of the pad of running feet in the grass behind her. Her body froze at the sound. When it came more clearly and was joined by a heavy panting, she glanced back over her shoulder with terrified eyes and saw the savage animal bearing down on her. The grayish-green beast with the glowing eyes was only a few yards distant from her!

CHAPTER 10

Lara raced on through the foggy night, sobbing in fear. Once she almost stumbled and fell. In that faltering second she was conscious of the phantom beast gaining on her and could almost feel its hot breath at the nape of her neck. Somehow she kept on and then she was at the bottom of the steps of the old house and Benson was standing in the open doorway. The little man's face registered terrified astonishment at the sight of her and the pursuing wolflike animal.

"Benson, help!" she gasped as she fell up the steps, collapsing in his arms.

The little man hurriedly dragged her inside and slammed the door closed. She leaned against the wall of the shadowed hallway, her breathing still labored.

Benson hovered nervously by. "Have you been injured, miss?"

She shook her head. "I'll be all right."

"That must have been one of those savage dogs Mr. Conrad has in the kennel," he said. "I always worry about them escaping. When I go by the enclosure they raise a dreadful row."

Lara was gradually recovering. "Where is Barnabas?"

Benson stood there uneasily. "He's down in the cellar yet," he told her. "He's seeing someone."

"I must speak to him at once."

"I'm sorry. I must ask you to wait," Benson said, sounding

worried.

She stared at him through the near darkness. "You don't understand. This is urgent."

"Mr. Barnabas has given me strict orders," Benson protested.

But Lara was too worked up to listen to such talk. Without giving the diminutive man a chance to argue further, she pushed by him and quickly made her way to the door that led to the cellar steps. Without hesitating, she went on down the uneven stone steps to the pitch blackness of the cellar. As she reached the earthen floor she was about to call out to Barnabas when a shocking tableaux was presented to her.

At the far end of the cellar a soft glow of flickering yellow candlelight showed through an open door. And silhouetted in the doorway was Barnabas Collins with a young woman in his arms. He must have heard her for he glanced down in the direction where she was standing and then said something in a low voice to the girl.

The two parted. And Lara saw the girl was one of the maids employed at Collinwood – a pretty, fair-haired girl, who had several times attracted her attention. Barnabas held the maid by the arm as he guided her part way across the cellar to a side set of steps that apparently led outdoors. The girl hurriedly mounted the steps and vanished. Then Barnabas came striding toward Lara, a troubled expression on his handsome face.

"You shouldn't have come down here!"

Lara was stunned. "I realize that," she said in a low voice.

His deep-set eyes had a tormented look. "If you're referring to that girl, it's of no importance. She came here from Collinwood with a message."

"I'm sorry I intruded," Lara said, near tears.

"Please, Lara," Barnabas begged. "You must have a little faith in me. I give you my word that girl means nothing to me in a romantic way."

Her eyes had wandered to the distant open door again. And she saw that the room beyond was furnished in an incredible fashion. An elaborate mahogany coffin was set up on stands and at either end of the coffin top silver candlesticks held burning black candles.

"What does all that mean?" she asked, indicating the room with a nod.

Barnabas sighed. "It has to do with my mission here. And it would take a long time to explain. I have not troubled you with it because I feel it has no importance to you."

His words stung her. Surely if two people were in love everything that concerned either of them was important to them both. Despite what she had seen, she wanted to believe Barnabas that the interlude had been an innocent one. But now he was reluctant to make reasonable explanations.

"Is that where you work?"

"I spend many hours in there," he said. "I'll show you the rest of the room later. Right now I want to take you upstairs and give you a sherry. You're trembling."

It was true. The discoveries in the cellar coming so soon after her frightening escape from the phantom wolf had left her in a highly nervous state. Too upset to argue further, she allowed him to shepherd her up the steep, stone steps to the hallway.

When she was seated in a chair before the blazing log fire in the living room sipping the sherry he'd given her, she began to feel better.

Barnabas looked at her with concern. "Are you more yourself now?"

"Yes."

He sighed. "You mustn't jump to conclusions about that girl or anything else you saw in the cellar. Those things have to do with a part of my existence which does not concern you."

"You mustn't keep on saying that," she pleaded with him. "I love you, Barnabas. And everything about you is important to me."

He gently touched her shoulder and looked down at her with tenderness in his haunted eyes. "If you love me, as you claim, you must have confidence in me. I will explain everything to you later. Believe that my feelings for you are deep and sincere."

"You're not making that easy," she murmured, "explaining nothing to me."

"I have my reasons. You must be patient. Finish your wine."

As the wine combined with the blazing logs to warm her and give her a feeling of well-being, she decided she should do as he asked – cling to her love and belief in him. She could hardly do anything else. He was the one she automatically turned to. And without him she would be facing the terrors of the gloomy old estate alone. She couldn't count on Michael Green; he was still almost a stranger to her.

She handed Barnabas her empty glass. "You know about Catherine's murder?"

"Yes," he said, taking the glass and carefully placing it on a nearby table. His back to her for a moment, he went on, "Who do they seem to suspect?"

"There has been all sorts of wild talk."

"I can imagine," Barnabas said coming back to stand facing her. "My guess is that it has to be Quentin."

She nodded. "I'm almost sure of it. His health seems very much worse. Of course he blames Conrad's dogs or even hints it was some wandering animal."

"Conrad won't much appreciate that," Barnabas said dryly.

"He's enraged," she agreed. "He suggests it could be that stranger, Michael Green, who did both killings. And because he wanted to cast suspicion on the dogs, he made them look like animal killings."

Barnabas raised his eyebrows. "What have you discovered about this Green?"

"Very little," she said. "Though we did meet this afternoon and I'll be seeing him tomorrow." She then mentioned the rendezvous they'd arranged for the following night.

"In the cemetery!" Barnabas pursed his lips. "I wonder why he chose that particular spot."

"He seems to go there often. It was there I first met him."

"He's a mystery," Barnabas said. "Yet I doubt that he is a murderer. Conrad has put forth that theory to protect his dogs."

"I agree," Lara said. "He's been reckless in his accusations." She paused a second. "He even hinted that you might be the guilty one."

The sallow, handsome face registered a grim smile. "I felt sure I would be included especially as Quentin is so anxious to be rid of me."

"I told them it was nonsense to talk like that about you."

"Thank you," he said quietly. "But I have an idea they didn't pay much attention to you."

"They're all acting slightly mad," she worried. "The odd thing is that Catherine came to me shortly before she was murdered and hinted she knew who killed Mary. And when I told her I wasn't in love with Quentin she promised to protect me."

Barnabas seemed interested. "Tell me more about the happenings at Collinwood. Beginning with Catherine calling on you and ending with your arrival here tonight."

She gave him a brief, rather breathless resume, concluding, "I think Quentin was about to take on the werewolf form as I argued with him. He looked ill as he tried to stop me from coming here to meet you. When he changed, he probably came after me with the idea of killing me."

"It suggests that," Barnabas agreed. "I don't suppose you had a good enough look at the animal to identify it again."

"No," she said, "though I think it was the one you shot at that other night. And I've noticed Quentin is still wearing a bandage on his right hand."

The flickering flames of the log fire cast a ruddy glow on his sallow face. "Things could get much worse," he warned her. "I may be dragged into this. Benson informs me the police chief called here today to question me."

"You needn't fear him," she said. "He's a stupid old man."

"His stupidity could be a threat in this instance."

"But he is convinced one of the dogs escaped and killed

Catherine just as one of them finished Mary."

"You're sure of that?"

"Yes," she said. "He probably only wants to ask you if you saw any of the dogs loose on the grounds that night."

"Perhaps," Barnabas agreed reluctantly.

"You could probably see him at the funeral tomorrow," she suggested. "I have an idea he'll be there if only to observe."

Barnabas frowned. "That's true. But I'll not be able to be present. I'll have to visit the grave later."

"It would be better if you showed up," she said. "Can't you make a single exception and appear?"

He shook his head sadly. "I very much doubt it. Though I would like to pay my respects to Catherine. It seems to me everyone has overlooked a very likely suspect in these crimes."

"Who?"

"Erica! That old woman may not be as senile as she pretends. She was a practicing witch and still may be. Especially in view of the things she has done on you. Many witches have been known to assume the wolf form."

She listened with a puzzled expression on her pretty face. "I dislike and distrust her," she said, "but I can't picture her as that snarling phantom beast."

He smiled thinly. "That could be her strength. You should be extremely cautious where she's concerned."

They talked on for more than an hour. Gradually she forgot about the upsetting incidents in the cellar, or at least lost her feeling that they had been important. She became absorbed in the several theories Barnabas had concerning the murders and his general attitude towards Collinwood.

He had come to sit beside her on one of the divans in the richly furnished room. "Collinwood has always had a strange hold on me," he confessed, "yet I have never known full happiness here."

She looked at him earnestly. "Why don't we leave here together?"

"We daren't consider that with things as they are now," he pointed out. "Quentin would be bound to blame the murders on me."

"Only to cover for himself," she said bitterly. "He's been trying to get me to say I'd marry him. I believe that's why he asked me here in the first place. But when he became more unwell he was so frightened he tried to halt my coming."

"It would have been better if you'd received that last letter," Barnabas said, his serious eyes fixed on her.

She gazed tenderly at his handsome, gaunt face and touched the lock of hair that straggled across his forehead. Again she was conscious of the coldness of his skin.

She said, "Your forehead is like your hands, icy!"

He was staring at her. "Does that frighten you?"

"It might in someone else. Not in you."

"Thank you," he said. "Those words mean more than you can know."

She was suddenly sad. "What's going to happen to us, Barnabas?"

"You'll leave here and lead a wonderfully happy life."

"I was asking about us," she reminded him gently.

He stood up. "It's time I took you back there," he said, "though I hate to do it."

She got to her feet and stared up at him worriedly. "I still think it would look better if you appeared at Catherine's funeral."

"I know," he said wearily. "I'll do what I can."

They kissed. But she had the feeling he was far away from her. The intimacy between them was lost. Her heart was heavy as he walked with her along the fog-shrouded path back to Collinwood. The night was oddly still except for the wash of the waves and the foghorn's wailing blasts. There was no sign of the monstrous beast which had been at her heels on her excursion to the old house.

Barnabas said goodnight at the door and she went inside. There was only a nightlight in the hall, a flickering candle in a wall bracket. She halted, gazing up at the dark portrait of the first Barnabas Collins for a moment. The face in the gold decorated frame was barely visible through the shadows.

How similar the Barnabas she knew was to that first Barnabas who had lived so long ago! Had their natures, too, been alike? What tragedy had caused him to leave Collinwood for distant England? Quentin had alluded to the long-ago Barnabas being considered a vampire, and had blamed the legend for making the present Barnabas unpopular in the village.

The walking dead! Someone had told her vampires were the walking dead. Her eyes narrowed as she stood there thinking about it. And then another association came into mind. Vampire bat! The tiny dead bat Erica had set out on her bedspread in a circle of blood was vivid to her memory. Had there been some special significance in the supposedly demented old woman's act? She had not tried to question her.

But now she began to feel the bat had meant something. Erica had placed it there for some purpose, perhaps related to Barnabas. Lara, suddenly tormented by the possibility, felt she should seek out the one-time witch and question her. Barnabas had warned her to be wary where Erica was concerned. But she felt she must take any risks necessary to discover additional information.

Slowly she mounted the dark stairs. She was deep in thought

and when she reached the landing on which her own room was located she did not stop, but went on up to the third floor where the old woman's quarters were.

At the door of Aunt Erica's apartment she paused for a moment. Then, very gently, she tried the doorknob. It turned under her touch and she cautiously swung the door open. The old woman's apartment assailed her nostrils with the musty smell of age and decay. But she forced herself to go on in.

The sparsely furnished living room was dark, but there was a soft light showing from a door down a short hall and on the left. Lara ventured on into the apartment and became aware of an even snoring from another room which revealed no light though the door was open. She decided the snorer was the housekeeper who'd taken over as companion to Erica.

The thought that these rooms had recently been the scene of a violent murder crossed her mind and she shuddered. Brushing aside the memory of Catherine's motionless body and torn throat, she forced herself to move slowly on to the lighted doorway. She was only a step from the doorway when she heard the low moaning sound.

It sent a chilling fear through her. And then she was staring into the bedroom lighted by a single candle on the dresser and saw the crouched figure of the ancient Erica seated on the side of her bed, wearing a long white flannel nightgown. Erica seemed not to see her at all.

Forcing herself to be calm, she went over to where old Erica sat staring into space and in a low voice said, "May I speak with you?"

The sharp, sunken eyes turned to her, revealing a gleam of triumph. "You!" Erica croaked.

"I need your help," she said earnestly. "Why did you place that bat on my bed?"

The old woman smiled craftily. "Because he is the one closest to you. He comes with eyes aflame."

Lara swallowed hard. "Had it anything to do with Barnabas?"

Erica looked off into space again and mumbled, "Black as night he stood. Fierce as ten furies, terrible as hell."

"Are you saying that Barnabas is a vampire?" she demanded anxiously.

"Demons there be!" Erica crooned with an ecstatic expression on her parchment, hawk face. "And Collinwood has known them all."

"What about Barnabas?"

Erica turned to her with scorn. "You will find out soon enough."

"Please!" Lara begged. "If you know anything, tell me."

But the old woman had turned into stone again, sitting there staring at thin air. It became apparent nothing would wake her from this strange condition. Lara also feared rousing the sleeping housekeeper. So with nothing accomplished she made up her mind to leave the room quietly. But just as she was about to turn and go her eyes caught the old woman's left hand which had been partly concealed from her. She caught her breath.

For neatly wrapped about the crone's hand was a narrow band of gray fur. Probably wolf's fur! And the stories of witches transforming themselves into werewolves by the act of wrapping a wolf's skin around them came rushing into her mind. It was plain that Erica was attempting to practice such black magic.

Or had she already successfully practiced it? Had it been she who'd changed into a werewolf and murdered Catherine? All the warnings Barnabas had given her came to mind. Trembling, she backed out of the room and then hurried through the darkness of the apartment. Not until she was in her own room with the bolt secured on the door did she feel any slight relief.

And long after she was in bed the eerie events of the night haunted her. And much of her thinking was about Barnabas. It seemed strange that lately she'd not had those vivid dreams in which he'd come to her bedside. She ran her fingers lightly across her throat, searching for some hint of the mark that had shown itself there slightly raised and swollen. It had vanished.

She finally dropped off into an uneasy sleep in which phantom wolf-like demons and a mad Erica pursued her. She tossed and murmured in her tortured dreams and when she awoke in the morning she was still weary and listless. But the day was fine. All signs of the fog had disappeared with the darkness. This was the day of Catherine's funeral.

Quentin, looking white and ill, approached her in the garden. "We will be leaving Collinwood for the cemetery at three-thirty," he told her. "The village undertaker is taking Catherine's casket directly to the cemetery. Because of her wounds the casket will not be opened."

"I understand," she said quietly.

He sighed. "It was the same with my late wife. I never saw Mary again after that awful sight of her on the beach."

Lara asked, "Will your great-aunt be attending the funeral?"

He looked grim. "No. Neither she nor Barnabas will be there."

She was surprised to hear him include Barnabas in his reply. "Are you certain about Barnabas?"

"Reasonably so," Quentin said bitterly. "He is fairly predictable. I assume you wish to attend."

"Yes, of course."

Quentin stared at her. "I'm sorry I was somewhat short with you last night. I wasn't feeling well."

"It didn't matter," she said quietly.

"I have no wish to interfere with you. You are here as our guest and you are free to do what you like . . . though I must admit I can think of companions I would be happier to see you with rather than my cousin Barnabas."

She furrowed her brow. "Why do you say that?"

"Because Barnabas is eccentric. Not suitable company for any young girl."

Lara smiled wanly. "I find him charming."

Quentin's sensitive face registered annoyance. "His charm is one of the dangers about him." And he abruptly walked away from her.

She stood there in the garden with its beds of roses. A soft breeze wafted in from the ocean to rob the warm sunlight of any unpleasantness. It was one of those perfect Maine days. To associate death and horror with such a day seemed impossible – but the main event of the afternoon was to be Catherine's funeral.

Lara strolled on toward the stables, head slightly bent. All at once she saw a girl coming from one of the barns with a basket of eggs on her arm. She was the blonde who'd been with Barnabas the night before.

Lara called out to her. "One minute!"

She halted with a questioning look on her pretty face. "Yes, miss?"

Lara hurried up to her. "I saw you at the old house last night."

The maid's blue eyes regarded her blankly. "Me, miss?"

"Yes. You must remember. You were in the doorway of the cellar room with Mr. Barnabas Collins when I arrived."

The girl showed uneasiness. "You must have me confused with someone else, miss."

"I can't have made a mistake," Lara protested. "I saw you clearly. You needn't be afraid to admit it. I mean you no harm."

"You saw someone else, miss," the girl said nervously.

"Your throat!" Lara exclaimed. "There's a red swollen mark on your throat just the same as the one I had on mine."

The maid seemed to consider her mad. She said, "It's a bite, miss. There are a lot of insects around at this time of year."

"But that's a different sort of mark," she argued. "Why were you with Mr. Barnabas?"

"I'm sorry," the girl said. "I didn't leave Collinwood last night. You surely are mistaking me for somebody else." And she quickly went on her way to the rear door and entered the house.

Lara stared after her in consternation. Either the girl was deliberately lying or Lara had made a stupid mistake. Yet she knew this was the identical girl she'd seen with Barnabas. Why had the maid been so vigorous in her denials? And what did that red mark on her throat mean?

Fearing that all this might bolster the theory that Barnabas was a vampire, Lara retraced her steps through the garden to the front of the house. It was time to dress for the funeral ceremony. And this was an experience she dreaded.

At three-thirty promptly she went downstairs in a suitable black silk dress. Quentin and Conrad Collins were there waiting for her in black mourning garb. Both men had a solemn, preoccupied air. Conrad merely nodded to her while Quentin came to her and asked, "Are you ready to leave?"

"Yes," she said in a small voice.

They all left the house together. It was a strange procession headed by Lara and Quentin Collins. Conrad Collins and the stout police chief came next. After that there was a group of the servants from the estate. They filed their way past the outbuildings as they walked to the family cemetery where the coffin of Catherine would be waiting by the open grave.

When the mourners reached the area of the kennels Lara was impressed by the fact there was no sound from the ugly big dogs behind its walls. They usually put on a fine show of rage and barking. But today it was as if they knew the procession had something to do with Catherine's tragic death. They were weirdly quiet.

In a low voice she remarked to Quentin, "Even the dogs seem aware we are on our way to a funeral."

"A funeral undoubtedly brought about by one of them," he said rather harshly.

She didn't pursue the subject. Soon the ancient burial ground at the foot of the hill came into sight. The pace of the group quickened a little as they neared the cluster of headstones and tombs inside the rusty iron fence. They found their way through the neat green mounds until they came to the newly dug grave where the elderly undertaker stood respectfully with his top hat in hand.

He quickly came over and shook hands with Quentin and Conrad Collins. "The coffin is here and ready," he said.

A clergyman Lara had not seen before appeared and began to offer a pious and flowery eulogy of the murdered young woman, which Lara considered in bad taste under the circumstances. She watched Quentin's face for a reaction. He showed none, just stood by the open grave listening with bowed head. Her eyes shifted to the other side of the grave and standing in the background was a newcomer. Someone she had never dreamed would be there. It was the stranger, Michael Green.

CHAPTER 11

A t once a series of wild conjectures ran through her mind. How had the stranger discovered the time of the burial? And how had he dared to show himself at the private funeral, knowing the Collins men resented him? Could he after all be the murderer there to witness the burial of his victim? She couldn't believe that.

It was more likely that he was there because of his admitted interest in the murders at Collinwood, and that he wished to show final respect for the lovely Catherine. Lara watched the coffin being lowered into the ground. When she raised her eyes again Michael Green was gone. There was no sign of him in the cemetery.

Quentin's angry voice, pitched low in her ear, demanded, "Did you see that fellow? He had a nerve to come here."

She turned to the upset young man. "You mean Michael Green."

"I had an impulse to go over and order him away," Quentin raged. "Only good taste prevented me."

"I'm sure he meant no harm."

Quentin's heavy dark brows raised in annoyance. "Merely being here was an affront to all of us." And he stalked away to stiffly greet the clergyman. Lara stood there unhappily, torn by confusion of feelings.

"Not a happy occasion, is it?" The question was put to her by Conrad Collins.

"No, it's all too dreadful!" she said, turning from the grave.

"May I walk you back?"

"I'd appreciate it," she said. "I can't stand being here just now."

"I know what you mean," he agreed quietly. And he took her arm and guided her away from the grave in the direction of the gate. "Quentin is in a mood about that stranger coming to the funeral."

"I can't see that it matters."

"Still, it was a brazen thing to do," Conrad said as he limped along at her side.

"He was very quiet and respectful."

"And he vanished before the service ended."

"I know."

"Could be he has a guilty conscience."

"I don't think so."

"Somebody murdered Mary and Catherine. Why couldn't it have been him?"

She sighed. "We've been over that ground before."

"And you don't believe it."

"No."

"You and Quentin would rather put the blame on my dogs."

She gave him a reassuring smile. "Please don't feel that way, Conrad. I'm not against you. And I don't hate your dogs. And I doubt if Quentin does. He's only attempting to be practical in the face of a situation he can't understand. A situation in which the dogs seem most likely to be guilty."

The young man looked unhappy. "None of my dogs were free on either night of the murders. I'd have known if they'd gotten loose. I've told that to Quentin and the police chief but they won't listen to me."

She had a sudden recollection of her flight from the mad, wolf-like creature the night before. She halted halfway up the hill and turned to him. "What about last night? Before I left the house I saw you going to the kennels with a lantern."

"I always do," he said. "I make a final check on them every night."

"Did you find a dog had escaped from the kennel last night?"

He frowned. "What are you trying to prove?"

"Answer me."

He regarded her uneasily. "When I went to the kennel every dog was there."

"Then your dogs can't be the killers!" she exclaimed.

It was his turn to show surprise. "Why do you suddenly decide that?"

"Because last night just after I saw you I was chased by a grayish-green brute. I barely escaped from it. If I hadn't reached the old house in time I don't know what would have happened."

Conrad eyed her queerly. "Have you talked to Quentin about this?"

"No."

"Why not?"

She searched for words to explain. She could hardly tell Conrad that she suspected his brother of being a werewolf and the murderer. "I haven't had an opportunity to. He was so busy with the details of the funeral today. In any case I'm sure it must have been a stray wolf or renegade dog."

"We know it wasn't one of mine," Conrad said. "That's all I care about. And I'll depend on you to tell him."

"Very well," she said, startled by the torment showing on his sensitive face. "If it means so much to you I will."

"You know how I feel about my dogs," Conrad said with great intensity. "They're out to make me destroy them."

"I'll tell Quentin what I've told you," she promised. "There's nothing more I can do."

Conrad further surprised her by taking a step nearer and seizing her by the arms. "Why do you hate me?"

"I don't," she protested. "Let me go. You're hurting me."

He continued to hold her in the savage grip. "You can't bear to have me touch you because I'm a cripple. That's it, isn't it?"

"You're wrong!"

"But you don't mind the touch of Barnabas," he raged on. "You don't worry about his cold hands or lips."

"Let me go!" she said, frightened by the wild look in his eyes.

"Barnabas, who consorts with the house maids and who never ventures into the sunlight! You admire him because he hasn't a deformed foot like me!"

"That's not true!"

He suddenly seemed to regain control of himself.

Staring at her in a dazed way for a few seconds he let her go. "I'm sorry," he said. "All the time you've been here I've been in love with you. And you despise me."

Her fear and anger swiftly melted into sympathy. She said, "You're terribly wrong about that. Actually I like you – better, perhaps, than Quentin. I'm sure you could be a fine man if you'd overcome feeling sorry for yourself and hating people."

Hope showed on his sensitive face. "I'll try, Lara. And then will I have a chance with you?"

Her tone was gentle. "I said I liked you, Conrad. But it is Barnabas I love."

Conrad looked grim again. "He is a handsome man," he said gruffly and resumed limping up the hill.

He was moving along so fast she had difficulty remaining at his side. She said, "I do want us to be friends."

"Do you think Barnabas will approve?" he asked sarcastically.

"Please don't be childish about this."

"It's all right," he said. But his tone was dull and he didn't look her way.

He kept on walking fast until they reached Collinwood. The strain of keeping up with him and contending with his difficult mood had completely wearied her. As soon as they entered the house she excused herself and went up to her room to rest.

She didn't appear again until dinner time. At the table she was careful to tell her story about being chased by the wild animal during a period when Conrad could vouch that none of the dogs were missing from the kennel. Quentin listened with cool disinterest and Conrad gave the impression that she hadn't presented the account to his satisfaction. As soon as he finished his coffee he sullenly excused himself and left her and Quentin alone.

Quentin waited until he had gone before saying, "My brother is in one of his difficult moods tonight."

"I tried to please him by telling you about that animal coming after me last night."

He smiled thinly. "You'll not find Conrad a grateful person. I never have."

As they got up from the table, she said, "There is something else I'd like to tell you. When I came in last night I went up to your Aunt Erica's apartment. I wanted to ask her some questions if she was awake."

Quentin looked stern. "I should think you'd want to avoid that mad old woman."

"She's not as mad as she pretends," Lara said. "I found her awake and I tried to question her. She gave me little satisfaction."

"That could be expected," he said as they stood in the shadowed dining room.

"But just before I left her I saw a strip of what appeared to be wolf's fur wound around her hand."

Quentin was startled. "Why do you tell me this?"

"Because I've read somewhere that witches used devices of that sort to make a transformation into werewolves. Knowing Erica's background of witchcraft, I wondered if she might be our murderer."

Quentin looked disdainful. "That's too utterly fantastic."

"You don't think it bears investigating?"

"No."

"I'd hoped the information might be of value," she said, feeling a keen disappointment at the manner in which he'd received her revelation.

Quentin looked stern. "I advise you to stay away from my aunt. She is quite mad and I cannot answer for her acts. That is why I moved you down to the second floor near me."

"I know," she said contritely.

"There's no point in Conrad trying to manufacture evidence of his dogs' innocence," Quentin went on. "Both the police chief and I agree that it has to be one of his dogs who is responsible."

"I see."

They moved on out to the hall where Quentin left her to go to his study. She went outside and found it still warm and pleasant. The sun was just going down. And she remembered that Michael Green had asked her to meet him in the cemetery between seven and eight. It was after seven now and although she dreaded entering the somber place where Catherine had been so recently buried she felt she should keep the appointment. He had promised to reveal more about himself and she was anxious to find out why he had chosen to appear at the burial.

Without returning to the house for her cloak, she took the path by the outbuildings and the old house where Barnabas lived. The vine-covered old house seemed deserted when she went by, but she had no doubt that Barnabas would show himself shortly. He usually worked until after sundown.

Going through the open gate of the quiet cemetery, she could hear the rustling of the tall pines in the forest just beyond. It gave her a strange sensation of loneliness. She thought how awful it was that two young women like Mary and Catherine should be the victims of some madman. Without meaning to she walked almost directly to Catherine's freshly-filled grave. She stood there staring down at the mound of black earth in silence.

And then she heard a sound of movement and lifted frightened eyes to see Michael Green showing himself from behind a broad, tall tomb. He came over to her.

"I felt it wise to hide until I was sure you were alone."

She studied him nervously. "You're right," she said. "There is a lot of resentment about your showing up here today."

He nodded. "I imagined there would be."

"Why did you do it?"

"I wanted to."

"That may be reason enough for you," she said. "But Quentin Collins would want you to have a better one."

Michael smiled bleakly. "I'm sure he would."

"You've taken a chance coming back here again tonight."

"I promised to meet you here."

"If you hadn't come I would have understood," she said. "Especially after your being here earlier, and them all seeing you."

"Just the same I'm very particular about keeping appointments," he said.

"So am I."

"I noticed that. I don't imagine you were delighted to come here so soon after the funeral."

"I wasn't."

"At any rate, we both kept our word." He sounded pleased.

"Not completely," she promptly replied. "You haven't told me why you are in Collinsport and you said you would."

"We had a close call at the beach." His eyes were on her, mocking her.

"You're avoiding the truth," she said. "Are you afraid of it?"

"Perhaps," the young man admitted. "But for a reason different than you suspect."

"I have only your assurance of that."

"I know."

"I wonder if it's enough."

His plain, pleasant face showed concern. "I'm hesitant to offer you too much information about me because it might expose you to danger."

"I'm willing to risk it."

"I don't know that I am."

"Please," she begged. "Be honest with me. As matters are now I don't know what to think about you."

He took a deep breath and stared at her in complete silence for a moment. "Have you ever heard of the Pinkerton Agency?"

Lara considered. The name had a familiar ring. Then she recalled what she knew about it. "Isn't that some sort of private detective agency?"

Michael Green's smile was bitter. "Right first time."

"And what has that to do with you?"

"You are unduly thick-headed this evening, Miss Balfour," he said. "I happen to be a Pinkerton agent assigned to investigate Quentin Collins."

Her eyes went wide. "By whom?"

"The parents of his late wife," he told her grimly. "They were by no means satisfied by the official investigation into their daughter Mary's death."

Lara stared at him. "You are telling me the truth, aren't you? This isn't some kind of fantastic lie?"

"I can show you my official badge if I must," he said in his mocking way.

"So that is why you are so interested in Collinwood; why you came here," she said in an awed voice.

"I only wish I could have saved her." He nodded at the new grave. "I feel that I have failed."

"You think Quentin murdered her as well?"

"Yes." His eyes met hers solemnly. "And my investigations have shown there were others."

"Others?" she asked, horrified.

He nodded. "At one time Quentin was courting a girl whose family have a fine home outside the village. She was found in the woods near her house dead from the attack of an animal. The verdict was that she'd been the victim of a wildcat. This was bolstered when an oversize wildcat was shot and killed in the area a few weeks later."

"But you think Quentin did it?"

"Yes." The young man's tone was grim. "Everything about that murder followed the pattern of these other two. Of course no one suspected Quentin at the time."

"You said others," Lara reminded him. "Was this girl the only one?"

"No."

"Who else?" She felt sickened at the news he was offering her.

"Quentin had been quietly seeing the daughter of a farmer who lives about ten miles from here. Not many people knew about it. But there was talk about this farmer's girl having been attacked and killed by the same wildcat. Her death came a few weeks before the other young woman's. I talked to the farmer and he was reluctant to give me any information at first. But in the end he broke down and admitted Quentin had secretly come to spend time with his daughter while he was engaged to the other girl. That was all I needed to know to convince me that the young master of Collinwood has left a trail of four murders behind him."

"When were the other girls. . ." She let the question fade unfinished.

"About a year after Mary died."

Lara regarded the young man with horror in her eyes. "What are you going to do now?"

He looked at her evenly. "Try to prove his guilt and save your life."

"Save my life?"

"Yes. There can be no question he has you marked as his next victim."

"I can't believe it! Why?"

"Because he's insane and afraid of you. He thinks you know too much. He'll go on thinking the same thing about every girl who catches his fancy until his murderous career is brought to a finish."

Lara moved away weakly, her head reeling. It was almost too much to grasp at once. She had suspected that Quentin was a murderer, but she'd had no idea of the extent of his crimes. This meant that even during the period when he'd been writing to her father about his music this young man had been a heartless killer. Yet in the light of his admiration for the lovely waltz her father had composed, this seemed incredible.

She halted beside a tomb and rested a hand against its cold marble for support. The distant whisper of the pines seemed to be mocking her, telling of evil at Collinwood still unknown to her.

Michael joined her with a troubled expression on his plain young face. "I hope this hasn't been too much of a shock. But you insisted on knowing."

"Yes." She smiled bitterly. "I insisted on knowing."

"The best course still might be for you to leave at once," he warned her. "Bringing Quentin to justice is not your responsibility."

"I have other reasons for remaining."

He frowned. "I think I know. Barnabas Collins."

She looked at him defiantly. "Why shouldn't I be in love with Barnabas?"

His eyes were sober. "I'd prefer to let Barnabas offer you his own arguments."

"Do you know something dreadful about him as well?"

"I haven't given him much time," the young man said. "I've been too busy trying to track down the facts about Quentin."

"But what do you know about Barnabas?"

He shrugged. "What the village people say."

"Yes?"

"That he's mad. And may be a vampire like one of his ancestors." The young man paused to smile thinly. "I may as well point out here that I'm not impressed by these legends of the supernatural."

"What do you believe?"

"That all the crimes here have been committed by human beings like you and me," he said shortly. "I've never encountered a case yet where the killer was some supernatural thing. And until I do I'll stay with my beliefs."

"How do you explain these bestial murders by Quentin?"

Green's face showed distaste. "Quentin takes insane fits. And he does the killings when he is in one of those fits. I don't even think he knows about what he's done afterwards – though I'd gather that by this time he's beginning to guess. That's why he's going around looking so pale and worried."

"He doesn't transform into a werewolf then?"

"I say no," Michael Green told her firmly. "I don't admit that werewolves exist. Unless you want to dub his insane mind the werewolf."

"And you think Barnabas could be mad in a different way?"

"There are many indications of it," the detective said. "Insanity likely runs through his entire family. The old woman is senile and crazy."

"Conrad is sensible enough," she pointed out.

"I wonder. He's sullen, and then there's his crazy obsession over those dogs. No sane man would train a pack of animals to be that wild."

Lara smiled bleakly. "You've made it all too simple. Everything is explained by the streak of Collins madness."

"Not quite, I regret to say." The words were spoken in the familiar cultured voice of Barnabas Collins.

Both Lara and Michael wheeled around to stare at him with surprise. The handsome man in the caped coat seemed to be enjoying the moment. Lara glanced up and saw that it was on the edge of dusk, the time that Barnabas usually showed himself. She'd been so caught up in the revelations of the Pinkerton man she'd not noticed the passing of time.

Moving forward to him, she said, "Barnabas! You're the last one I expected."

"Benson told me he saw you coming down this way," he said. "And he was worried that you hadn't come back. I felt I should find out why."

Gratitude showed on her lovely face. "I'm glad you did." She turned to Michael. "This is a Pinkerton man sent by the parents of Quentin's first wife to investigate the murder of their daughter."

Barnabas regarded the young man blandly. "You seem to have arrived at a very poor opinion of the entire Collins family."

Michael looked unhappy. "I'm sorry," he said. "I spoke too quickly. I'm sure that I was mistaken."

"You are if you believe me insane," Barnabas said casually, "in spite of what the ignorant villagers claim."

Michael spread his hands. "You must admit you don't behave normally by their standards."

"You are quite right," Barnabas said smoothly. "However, it happens that my standards are not theirs."

"I realize that. I guess I owe you an apology."

Lara smiled at Barnabas. "I say you should accept it."

"I fully intend to," he said. "It happens that this young man's purpose here is similar to my own. We both want to save you from Quentin and his lunacy."

Michael Green was quick to pick this up. "Then you are willing to admit your cousin is insane."

Barnabas eyed him somberly. "He could be worse than that. I know you are skeptical about the supernatural, but I have lived a good deal longer than you. I know there are things not fully understood by normal humans."

"I'll have to reserve my opinion on that."

"By all means," Barnabas told him. "It seems you have delved deeply into Quentin's deeds up until now. But what interests me most is how you plan to trick him into revealing himself as a murderer."

Michael glanced at her. "I guess I hoped that Lara might be willing to remain here and offer herself as bait."

The young man's words sent a chill through her but she had no thought of refusing to help him. "Do you think that will work?"

"I'm almost positive of it," the young detective said.

Barnabas frowned. "I trust you're remembering the cost of such a scheme for Lara if anything should go wrong."

"I'm not likely to forget it," Michael said with a troubled look her way.

"The weakness of it all," Lara said, "is that Quentin is even now wary of me."

"I don't think that will matter," the detective said.

Dusk had cast a blue glow over the scene. Lara thought how unreal it was; the three of them standing together beside the ghostly white tomb in the old cemetery, calmly discussing how to make the suspected murderer betray his true self.

Barnabas broke the short silence. "There is a full moon tomorrow night. It will be the most difficult time for Quentin to control his murderous impulses."

"That's true," Michael Green said. "We should make our move then. The longer we hold off, the more danger for Lara."

"If Lara goes to him tomorrow night," Barnabas went on, "the chances are he'll make an attack on her. Providing he is the guilty person. And I think he is."

"There is a balcony outside his study windows," Michael said. "I've been making note of the layout of the house. You and I could wait out there to be ready to come to Lara's assistance."

Barnabas nodded. "He usually goes to his study for an hour or two in the early evening."

Michael turned to her. "You don't have to agree. But if you go to him with some questions, or any other pretense, it would give us the ideal chance to test him."

"I'll do it," she said. "I owe that much to Catherine."

"I don't think you owe anything to anyone," Barnabas said. "But I do believe it would be to everyone's benefit to get this settled."

"And the proof must be positive to convince the local authorities," the young detective grumbled. "I've found them thick-headed."

Barnabas said, "Are you sure you want my help? I could be the murderer."

Michael smiled. "I'm willing to risk that."

"Then it's settled," Barnabas said. "I'll meet you at the old house about dusk. Then we can proceed to Collinwood and station ourselves by the study window."

"So you mustn't venture near Quentin until after dark," Michael warned her.

"I understand."

"Even waiting out there, we might not be quick enough if what I expect to happen does happen," Barnabas said slowly.

Michael Green frowned. "Just what do you expect to happen?"

"You're much too skeptical to believe me if I told you."

Lara gazed directly at Barnabas and said, "I know what you're thinking. You believe in the gypsy curse that was put on Quentin. You think he has really become a werewolf."

"Yes," Barnabas said grimly. "I do."

CHAPTER 12

Barnabas' awesome declaration caused them to be silent again. A gull that had winged in from the bay flew over their heads giving out with its familiar melancholy cry. The unexpected sound made Lara start. The conference in the deserted cemetery had left them all tense.

Michael Green said, "That's about all we can settle now. I'd best be moving on. I have other things to do."

Barnabas nodded. "Until tomorrow night, then."

"Yes."

Lara warned the detective, "You should leave the estate at once. They're watching for you. And it could be bad if they found you here."

He smiled at her. "Thanks for worrying about me." He appeared about to leave them, but he hesitated. "There is one other thing."

"What?" she asked.

"You don't have any weapon to protect yourself."

"I haven't needed one."

"You might now." From inside his coat he drew out a small gun and handed it to her. "This is tiny enough to hide in a dress pocket and yet deadly enough to take care of you. I want you to keep it with you all the time. It's loaded and ready to use."

She held back from accepting it. Turning to Barnabas, she said, "What do you think?"

"I say you should take it. And use it the moment you decide you're in danger."

Lara turned back to the young man again. "Very well."

He gave her the gun. "I'll feel easier knowing you have that."

She stared down at it. "I doubt if I can use it properly."

"Aim and fire," Michael told her. "The chances are in your favor you'll do some damage." He turned to Barnabas. "You'll see her back to Collinwood safely?"

"Yes."

"Then I'll be on my way." Michael quickly walked off toward the gate and was lost in the shadows and forest of tombstones.

Now that they were alone Lara turned to Barnabas. "I was so glad you came when you did," she confided. "It changed everything."

"You appeared to be getting along very well with that young man."

"To think he's a detective! A Pinkerton man!"

"I've suspected that for quite a while," Barnabas told her. "It was logical that Mary's parents would want to find out more facts about their daughter's tragic death."

"I can't get used to having this," she said, holding up the gun.

"Put it in your dress pocket as he advised. Then try not to think about it until you have a need for it."

"I hope that won't happen."

"You must be prepared."

She obeyed him, placing the small weapon in the pocket of her full skirt. It fortunately didn't show there and it would be easy for her to reach for it. She shivered. "It's getting cold here."

"I know," he said. "We'll walk back to my place." Along the way he questioned her about the happenings since he'd seen her. And she filled him in on the various events as well as she could. On reaching the house they went to the living room and he poured her out a generous glass of the sparkling ruby sherry.

She stood with it before the fireplace and watched the reflection of the flames in the glass. "You don't ever have a sherry with me."

"I have no taste for wine," was his comment. "Your mention of Erica and the strip of wolf's fur surely has some meaning in all this."

"You think so?"

"I've always thought so," Barnabas said. "It is still possible we are dealing with a murderess rather than a murderer. Quentin may be proven innocent."

Lara stared at him incredulously. "I still can't picture that frail old woman as a snarling huge beast."

"Because like Michael Green you don't fully accept the fact of lycanthropy. You do not think humans can transform themselves into animals and back again."

"I suppose not," she admitted.

He frowned. "I'm bound to accept the supernatural. I have seen too many strange things not to. So there we differ. But perhaps tomorrow night will settle our doubts."

She sipped her wine. "I hope so. I'd like to get it over with." She gave him an appealing look. "Can we leave as soon as the murders are solved?"

"You will be able to."

"But I won't go unless you come with me," she told him. "I love you, Barnabas."

He smiled sadly and touched his cold lips to her cheek. "We will go into all that later."

Lara glanced around the dark room with its elegant furnishings. "This is a lovely old house and Collinwood is even more impressive. But I don't want to ever see either of them again."

"I can understand that."

She eyed him worriedly. "Would you mind a great deal if you were never able to return?"

Barnabas looked surprised. "I have never thought about that. It has always seemed so natural for me to be here. I am part of Collinwood in a very real sense."

"Of course that is so true," she worried. "I hate to ask you to give it all up. Perhaps you could make short visits here on your own occasionally."

The handsome face showed amusement. "I'd say you'll make a truly generous wife."

"I want to," she told him earnestly. "I want to be a perfect wife to you, Barnabas." She moved away from him, her partly filled wine glass in hand, to inspect some of the ornaments scattered about the room. She paused to admire a teak Buddha that had undoubtedly been carved in China long ago by some talented but forgotten artist. Clipper ships had brought the treasures of every land back to the mariners' homes in Maine.

On another table she found a brass vase from India. The pattern was intricate and it looked extremely valuable. And beside it was an ivory tile, about two inches square, with the likeness of a male face. She lifted the tile and to her delight found that it was a pen drawing of Barnabas.

She turned to him with the tile in her free hand. "This is wonderful!"

Barnabas looked pleased. "It's rather old."

Lara studied it again. "You haven't changed at all. And it looks as if you were wearing a coat of the same cut."

"Very likely."

She sighed. "This is the sort of thing I prize. When we leave here, Barnabas, let us gather up all the treasures I feel I can't do without and take them with us."

"If you wish," he said. "All the things in this house were left to me. We'd be well within our rights."

"Then that's what we'll do," she said happily as she put the tile back on the table. "When we have a home of our own, that drawing of you will hold a prized place."

"I'd much prefer having an artist do a likeness of your lovely face," he told her.

She went across the room to him and he placed an arm around her and gently touched his lips to hers. In that blissful moment she was able to forget all the problems they faced, all the dangers she must brave until the crimes that had taken place at Collinwood were solved. All that mattered was that she loved Barnabas and was in his arms.

When he let her go, he said, "I must soon get you back to the main house. Quentin will be getting suspicious."

"He's that already," she said. "He doesn't like me coming here or seeing you."

"That is why I seldom enter Collinwood," Barnabas confided. "Our being together always produces more bad feelings. So I have given up seeing him completely."

"He is very difficult to get along with," she said. "He and Conrad are almost always at odds."

"A nasty situation," Barnabas agreed. "Perhaps another generation will see Collinwood a happier place."

She eyed him with surprise. "You often come out with strange comments."

The gaunt, handsome face showed embarrassment. "Do I? I'm sorry. I don't mean to."

They left the old house soon after that and he saw her to the front entrance of Collinwood. Before he left her, he reminded her, "Don't forget you have that gun. And don't be afraid to use it."

"I'm almost more frightened of it than anything else," she confessed.

"You mustn't take that attitude," he said. "It is your best protection. And you may need it badly before another twenty-four hours pass."

"I'd remember," she promised. But it still was like a bad dream to her.

When she awoke in the morning the sunshine of the previous day had vanished. It was dark and threatening once more, a dull gray morning that matched her mood. She selected another dress with a pocket in the skirt so that she could continue to keep the gun by her. But already she was beginning to feel she would never need the weapon.

Conrad suggested she might enjoy a drive into the village with him. "I've got to go in and see our lawyer about one of the farm deeds," he explained. "The tenants are always giving us trouble."

The idea of getting away from the old house even for a short while was appealing to her. She said, "I'd enjoy the drive, but what if it should rain?"

He smiled. "My carriage has a top. And there are sides to fasten on if it should rain really hard. But I doubt if we'll need them. We won't be gone all that long."

"How soon do you want me to be ready?"

"In about twenty minutes," he told her. "I'll bring the carriage around to the front and wait for you."

She went upstairs to get her cloak. She hadn't seen Quentin all morning and guessed that perhaps he was ill and because of this had remained in his room for breakfast. He sometimes did. When she was in her own room she listened for some sound from the adjoining room which he occupied but heard none.

Conrad's carriage was very smart and painted a shiny black. It had a gray fringe around the top of which he was duly proud. The two dappled gray horses completed the picture. He lifted the reins as soon as she joined him on the carriage seat and they were off to Collinsport at a fast trot.

Conrad seemed to be in an excellent humor. He told her, "Quentin has just about made up his mind to put Aunt Erica in the state asylum. And I say that is where she belongs."

Not being one of the family, Lara hesitated, then contented herself with saying, "She is a very strange old woman."

"A witch!" Conrad said grimly. "She brought about my father's death. And it could be she had something to do with what happened to Mary and Catherine."

"Do you think so?" she asked. "But then there were the deaths of those other two girls Quentin knew."

Conrad glanced at her quickly. "How did you find out about them?"

She felt her cheeks crimson. The information had slipped out without her realizing. She knew she'd made a bad blunder. And she desperately hoped it wouldn't lead to a suspicion of Michael Green.

She hurried to say, "Quentin mentioned it to me."

"Quentin did?"

"Yes."

Conrad returned to giving his attention to guiding the horses. "I'd expect that would be the last thing he'd want to talk about. In any case, those girls were both killed by a wildcat that was shot down soon after. That cat was a regular monster."

"So I've heard." Trying to change the subject, she began to comment on the rugged scenery along the shore. Conrad agreed with her in an absent fashion, but she worried that she'd gotten him thinking about the murders.

Little was said between them the rest of the way to the village. She waited in the carriage while he was in the lawyer's office. And then when he came out he took her for a short shopping tour of the tiny stores on the steep main street. The clouds continued to gather and she was relieved when they began the drive back to Collinwood. Conrad began to question her about her own background and where she'd lived. She was glad to keep him on the subject and it occupied most of the drive back.

They were within sight of the sprawling old mansion with the many tall chimneys when it began to rain. She saw the first drops and said, "How lucky! We're getting back before the storm really begins."

Conrad nodded. "I didn't expect it any sooner. It will probably rain all evening and through the night now. This is the kind of weather that makes it nasty for the night boat."

"It was very foggy and wet the night I arrived."

"It can be bad."

"How many times does the night boat visit here?"

"She brings passengers and cargo three nights a week," Conrad said. "And she's due tonight."

"Barnabas met me when I arrived," she recalled. "Otherwise I don't know what I would have done."

Conrad frowned. "I don't know why Quentin didn't mention your coming to me. I'd have been glad to go to the village and meet you."

"Remember? He thought I wasn't coming."

"That's what he claims."

He brought the carriage to a halt at the front entrance and helped her down. The rain was getting heavier and she was glad to hurry to the door and go inside. She was on her way to the stairs when Quentin came down the corridor to greet her with a frown.

"Where were you?" he wanted to know.

"Conrad took me to the village for a drive," she said, at once aware that he was in one of his tense moods.

"I worried about you," he said accusingly. "You should have mentioned where you were going to someone."

"I didn't think it was that important."

"What did Conrad want to talk to you about?" Quentin demanded. "I suppose he was talking behind my back as usual."

"No," she said. "We talked mostly about my life back home. And about my father."

Quentin's lip curled. "He was just pretending to be interested in you. He doesn't even like your father's music."

"We didn't discuss music," she said, somewhat hurt.

"Whatever Conrad said, you mustn't pay any attention to it," Quentin went on angrily. "He hates me and he's always scheming against me."

Lara looked at his enraged face and felt a kind of despair. "I didn't think I'd be making trouble for either of you when I accepted his invitation."

Quentin looked a trifle less upset. "I've only tried to warn you for your own good."

"Thank you," she said quietly and she went on upstairs.

She could tell that the tension between the brothers was reaching a danger point. Anxious not to become involved in the dispute, she decided to remain in her own room until dinner time.

In the late afternoon she managed a small nap and felt much better as she dressed for the evening meal. Again she was forced to select a gown with a suitable pocket to conceal the gun. She wondered what either of the brothers would do if they suspected she was carrying a weapon.

The rain had gotten heavier. There would be no full moon visible; she wondered if she should go through with the agreed-upon plans. She decided that she should. Surely Michael Green would have found some way to get word to her if he wanted her to change tactics.

Somehow she got through dinner with the two brothers, who were barely speaking to each other. As soon as the meal was over she went into the living room and sat with a book. Every so often she glanced out to see that it was still raining. She was waiting for darkness and the moment when she would go to Quentin's study and get his reaction.

One of the maids came in and lighted the lamps in the chandeliers. Lara continued to read. She heard footsteps in the hall and saw Conrad leaving by the front door in black raincoat and brimmed rubber hat. He was carrying a lantern as usual. He would be making his late night visit to the kennels.

She forced herself to read on some more. She didn't dare rush things. It was important that Barnabas and Michael be posted outside before she entered Quentin's study. And she worried that they might be uncomfortable out there in the driving rain.

Her eyes were on the printed page of the book she held, but she was not really taking any of it in. She was much too nervous. Then suddenly from upstairs she heard the high-pitched mad laughter of Aunt Erica, and a stream of reprimand from the housekeeper, who had apparently caught her trying to escape downstairs.

Lara looked up from the book and felt a chill slide down her spine. She pictured the mad old woman. Was Erica still practicing her witchcraft? Was she really more powerful than any of them in spite of her seeming weakness? It was a troubling question. The memory of that wolfskin lingered to torment Lara.

Silence had returned to the house again temporarily. Then from the study she heard the muffled sound of Quentin's gramophone and the tune was her father's waltz. It was almost like a cue for her. Mind made up, she put the book aside and rose from her chair. She touched a hand to the pocket containing the gun and then left the living room to walk slowly down the shadowed hallway to Quentin's study.

The door was shut with the music still playing inside. She knocked on the door but he didn't seem to hear. So she knocked again, louder this time. After a moment he opened the door and looked startled to see her standing there.

She apologized, "I heard the waltz and decided to come down here."

"Oh," he said, with a slight frown. "Yes. The waltz."

"It is a lovely tune," she said, entering the study. "I think it's perhaps the best thing my father ever wrote."

Quentin nodded. Then he went over to the gramophone and turned it off. "It's difficult to talk through the music."

A silence fell between them. She looked at his pale, handsome face, remembering how much his letters had meant to her father in his final sickness.

"Somehow it's always been difficult to talk – for us, I mean," she said slowly, hoping he would understand how sorry she suddenly felt about the way things had turned out.

"Lara," he said hesitantly. "You've always been the waltz to me – graceful and beautiful, and with a promise of a happier life than mine. I once thought – "

She saw that his hands were trembling and he looked extremely pale and ill. She said, "Is there something wrong?"

He touched a hand to his temple. "My head again. It's very bad." And he bent slightly, staggering and clutching the desk with a hand to keep himself from falling.

Lara fought her panic. "Is there anything I can do?"

"No!" It was more like a groan than a reply. He seemed to be writhing in pain and he bent down over the desk once again.

And then she saw the change that was coming over him. It had begun in his hands. They were no longer human hands. The long hair on them was a grayish-green, the same color as the monster that had attacked her the other night. And as she drew away from him she saw the change was also taking place in his face. Hair had sprouted on his cheeks until the white skin was covered and his teeth had become fierce animal fangs. The tortured eyes of a few moments ago had changed to an eerie amber. And this thing that Quentin had become was crouched before her snarling and ready to spring in attack.

Lara screamed and dug in her pocket for the gun. Whipping it out she fired it point-blank. The bullet found its mark; the werewolf fell back with blood spurting from its body. Then with an unearthly howling it bounded towards the French windows and burst out into the darkness and rain, leaving a trail of blood across the floor.

Lara's head was spinning and she let the gun drop from her nerveless fingers to the carpet. At the same instant one of the walls of books swung open, revealing a secret door. Conrad Collins stood there smiling in a mad, evil way as he restrained a wild, slavering Caesar by holding onto his collar.

"I've been waiting for this moment," he told her. "It's always been Caesar and me. And Quentin thinks he's to blame."

Lara was back against the wall, terror shadowing her lovely face. She stared at the crippled man with wide horrified eyes. "You're the one responsible for all those murders. You and Caesar!"

Conrad nodded malevolently. "I decided on it when Quentin began taking his spells. He's never killed anyone. But he thinks he has! Soon he'll kill himself or the authorities will get him. And then I'll have Collinwood!" He bent close to the poised, snarling animal. "Her throat, Caesar!"

Lara made a vain attempt to regain the gun on the floor as the great dog came bounding at her. But she didn't manage it and then she felt the impact of its body against her. She was also vaguely aware of a shot close at hand. There was a mournful whining from the big animal as it quivered, fell and then lay motionless on the floor. She looked up and saw Barnabas and Michael advancing to her.

From the door of the secret passage Conrad screamed, "You've killed Caesar!" Then he turned and vanished in the darkness as Michael fired a shot after him.

Barnabas said, "I'll go after him. You remain here with her." And he entered the secret passage.

Michael helped her into one of the big leather arm chairs. And then he stared at the dead Caesar with revulsion. "What a twisted maniac that Conrad is to teach a dog to be a killer!"

She nodded weakly. "He claimed he did all the murders with Caesar."

"I don't doubt it." He glanced at her again and crossed over to the sideboard. "You need some brandy."

"What about Barnabas?"

"He'll manage," Michael assured her. "He'll be more than a match for Conrad." And he came back to her with a small glass of brandy. "Try that."

The brandy burned her mouth and throat, but it helped clear

her head. "What now?"

He shook his head. "I don't know. In spite of the way Quentin ran out of here you must have hit him in some vital spot. Look at that blood on the carpet! He'll probably die somewhere out there." The young man grimly turned his attention to the dead Caesar. "And so our werewolf turns out to be a wild dog directed by a madman!"

Lara stood up and stared at him. "Didn't you see?"

"What?"

"Quentin, when he left," she said in an awed voice.

He shook his head. "I couldn't get a look inside because of the drapes. And when he bounded out I didn't have a chance. Conrad had just appeared on the scene to take our attention."

She bit her lip nervously before she said in a near whisper. "He changed. I saw it. Turned into a kind of wolf-like monster."

Michael regarded her sympathetically. "Don't try to think about it. It was probably your imagination anyway."

"It wasn't!" she protested. And then she said, "You don't believe me!"

"Sorry," he said. "But it's my guess when we find Quentin's body out there with your bullet in it we'll find the body of an ordinary man."

"No," Lara whispered. "No!" Her vision blurred again. What had she done? Quentin – the man who had loved her father's waltz, who had loved her, perhaps . . . Had she killed him in what could have been her own hysterical delusion? But she had seen him change, hadn't she? Then why hadn't Michael seen it? Now, she thought, I am fighting for my own sanity. But Michael was saying something.

"It doesn't matter. According to his brother, Quentin had those mad spells but he didn't do any of the killings."

Lara turned and saw Barnabas coming back into the study through the French windows. This time he closed them carefully after him before he announced, "Conrad is dead. I chased him to the cliffs and he hurled himself over."

Michael said, "So the case is closed."

"Not quite," Barnabas told them grimly. "There is still Quentin out there. And with a bullet from that gun." He nodded to the floor.

Lara asked him, "What will we do?"

"I've decided that," Barnabas said with crisp authority. "There's going to be a lot of explaining to do and I can handle it best alone. With you two out of the way it will merely be a case of the brothers having a fatal quarrel over the shooting of Caesar. It ended with Conrad shooting Quentin and then killing himself."

Michael seemed to follow this. "It could be easier with us gone," he agreed.

"We'll assume all this happened after you left on the night boat," Barnabas said. "It docks here within the hour. And as soon as you two are safely on board I'll report what has gone on here to the police."

Lara ran over to him. "No. I won't leave you!"

"It's only for a little while," Barnabas said gently. "Go upstairs and pack the bare necessities for the trip. You can get your other things later."

She knew he would persuade her and he did. The ride to the village, with Barnabas at the reins of the carriage continuing to calmly tell them what to do, seemed nightmarish.

The rain was coming down as heavily as before when they stood on the wharf to say goodbye. The nightboat had landed her cargo and passengers and was now taking on some freight. In a few minutes the big side-wheeler would be churning off into the darkness.

There were tears in Lara's eyes. "Come with me."

Barnabas smiled at her. "I'll see you again in a short while." He kissed her gently. "Take care of her for me, Michael."

"I'll do my best," the young man promised. "Good luck, Barnabas." And then he hurried Lara on board the ship just before the gangplanks were taken in.

Despite the rain, Lara made her way up to the open deck and tried to spot Barnabas on the wharf. The side-wheeler was a short distance from the shore now and with the rain and only the few torches to light the wharf it was hard to see. She thought she saw his ramrod-straight figure standing alone there but she could not be sure.

Michael was at her elbow. "Better come inside. You're getting drenched."

When they were in the warm, softly-lighted main salon Lara looked at him despairingly and asked, "Is it going to be all right? What about Barnabas?"

"He'll manage."

"He didn't say when I'd see him again or where," she lamented. "Nothing was settled."

The young man's tone was sympathetic. "He did give me something for you earlier in the evening. In the excitement I forgot it." And he reached in his pocket and drew out the small tile with the drawing of Barnabas on it. "He said it was for you." He paused and then went on gently. "He asked me to tell you he can never see you again. And he prefers that you don't question the reasons."

Her eyes brimmed with tears as she studied the sad, handsome face on the tile.

Coming Soon From Hermes Press

...and more thrilling *Dark Shadows* editions!

ᴅARK ᴊHADOWS

Published by **Hermes** Press

Dark Shadows: The Complete Series: Volume 1
SECOND EDITION
From the Gold Key Comics 1968-1970
www.hermespress.com

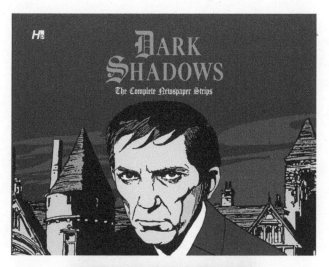
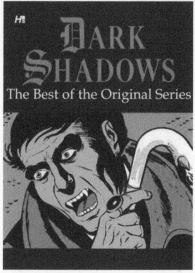